That's Entertainment

That's Entertainment

stories

Robert Neilson

ELASTIC PRESS

This collection is dedicated to
Stacey, Vickie, Danielle, Christopher and Lily.
My family.
So far.

Table of contents

That's Entertainment

"Superman was always a bastard."

"You can't say that."

"It's my autobiography. In my head, it's always started with that line."

My fingers hovered over the keys of my laptop like flies with a sudden aversion to dead meat.

"He never liked me, you know. I was supposed to be in *Action* one-oh-nine but somehow it never happened. The writers changed their minds at the last minute. So I was told. But I knew it was that simpering blue-haired bastard. He nixed it. It would have been my big break. Instead I ended up as second banana in a *Dark Spectre* issue for King Features. Three fan letters mentioned me by name, but I never got another gig with King.

"My image was too challenging for them. I was just too radical for the forties. Nobody wanted to take a chance on a guy with subliminal gender issues. That's what they called it, you know. You think political correctness started in the nineties? They just gave it a new name. Everything got a new name."

All of a sudden he had nothing to say, an empty husk now the words had fallen out. It had taken me ages to get him to start talking; now I was hoping he'd stay silent. Then I could just go home. Tell my boss he wouldn't talk. How can you ghost write for a psychotic? Or whatever the hell he is? It was hard enough to take him seriously when he answered the door in an orange gingham dress. I couldn't help but stare at the knotted veins in his pipe-cleaner legs; the puffy blue ankles; the fluffy pink slippers that screamed at the dress. The temptation had been to cut and run, but I really needed the commission. What sort of a professional would I be to let an old guy in a dress weird me out.

He combed a skeletal hand through his sparse white hair, pushing it away from his forehead like a Hollywood ingénue angling her best side into shot. "You must be Andrew." He stepped away from the door and ushered me inside. "Drop your bag there. We'll get you squared away later."

The house was about the size of an average three-bed-semi but it seemed to have about a hundred little rooms, hardly any of them bigger than a walk-in closet. He led me to a tiny kitchen and insisted on making tea – he had Earl Grey and I had Irish Breakfast. "You a fan of my work, Andrew?"

I was a fan of the four grand my editor at Endale Press was offering for the job.

"I've never even heard of Forbes Tyler."

Joe Grennan was a tyrant of the old school. He knew my weakness – eating/rent/the odd pint – and was well aware that my wage habit had gone unsupported for several weeks. "Jesus, kids. You never read comics?"

"When I was twelve."

Grennan's eyes got that faraway look as he stared over my left shoulder into that faraway present where he was still young. "Forbes Tyler, The Grey Ghoul."

"What the hell is The Grey Ghoul?"

"He was in colour in the sixties and seventies. The Green Ghoul?" I shook my head.

"You've got a lot of research to do between now and ten tomorrow morning. Don't let me keep you."

I was dismissed. If Grennan spoke to me again it would be in a roar. 'I don't like to boil my cabbage twice,' he said to me the first time we met. Boy, was that an understatement. With Joe Grennan you got it the first time or you didn't work.

go," he said. "Apparently we're short of early morning shots of the Philistines' camp. You better get going too. Don't want you pair fouling the shot as you saunter over to the big fellow's tent."

"I wasn't aware there was anything on this morning for me to foul up," Woolfe said.

"That's the thing about character liaison," Hank said. "Always last to hear."

"Come on, Denny," Woolfe said. "I've managed to scrounge a jeep. The new director arranged it for me. Matter of professional courtesy. Being an ex-someone has its good points."

They drove out of the encampment on a rutted dirt road. The small valley that had been chosen as the outside broadcast unit's operations centre was well away from the battleground or the warring factions' camps. Although he had been briefed on what to expect on this trip nothing could have prepared him for his first sight of the Philistine camp. It was spread out across the plain from the foot of the mountain as far as the eye could see. Not only was there the expected sea of tents but there were uncountable wagons and baggage animals and there seemed to be sheep everywhere. As they drove up Denny could see at least five individual flocks each numbering in the thousands.

Everywhere there was a buzz of activity. It was as if the life and commerce of an entire province had been uplifted and dropped into a tented city in the desert. He could see various types of produce being laid out in front of some of the tents, as the merchants opened for business. He was surprised at how little attention was being paid to their transport, though when he thought about it the production had been preparing to shoot the upcoming confrontation for over a year. They regularly passed the large screens that had been set up throughout the camp so that the participants could see the results of the filming. Whether these people actually understood the concept behind television or not, all of them were keen to see themselves on the screen. Right from the early days of historical programming it had always been the easiest way to persuade people to perform for the cameras. Everyone wanted to be a star.

The jeep pulled to a halt outside a large, ornate tent guarded by two sentries, one of whom disappeared inside as soon as the jeep came into sight. "This is it," Woolfe said. He placed a hand on Denny's shoulder preventing him from getting out of the jeep. "Don't make the mistake of underestimating this guy. He may look like he's just brawn, but from all reports he's a pretty shrewd character. The king's champion is a political appointment as much as a military one. Remember, history is written by the winners, so you couldn't expect Goliath to have come out of it smelling of roses."

One sentry pulled aside the flap of the tent as they climbed out of the jeep; the other signalled them inside with his spear. "I guess we're expected," Woolfe said.

Goliath sat on an enormous chair, almost like a throne. He was indeed a huge man but nowhere near the ten feet that the Bible claimed. Denny guessed he was maybe seven six or seven eight. His musculature was spectacular but yet again Denny was surprised at the amount of flab he carried at his middle.

Smiling broadly through a thickly curling black beard, Goliath waved for them to sit on a collection of skins and rugs at his feet. "I have waited to break my fast with you," he said. His speech was slow and precise. Despite an accent that rolled out the Rs indefinitely and inserted something like the preparation for spitting into most words, he was relatively easy to understand. "Do not be alarmed," he continued, "there are no unusual delicacies. Your friends, who were here before you, have coached me in what you English like to eat."

"It is kind of you to consider our tastes," Woolfe said. "Please allow me to introduce myself and my colleague. I am Ernest M. Woolfe and this is Denis Mantle."

Goliath grunted. He stared hard at Woolfe for a couple of moments assessing him, then turned his gaze onto Denny. "What shall I call you?"

"Denny's fine," Denny said.

"And you'd better call me Ernie."

He clapped his hands impatiently. "Where are those girls?"

Three female servants entered from the rear of the tent carrying trays of food and hurried to serve breakfast. Denny couldn't help but notice that each of them was young, slim and beautiful. None of them would meet his eyes.

"I see you like my slaves," Goliath said.

Denny blushed and tried to work out what sort of a reply was expected.

Goliath laughed. "You have such wonderfully strange customs," he said. "If it is not an insult, or against your beliefs, you may choose one for yourself. She would be yours whenever you are here and for as long as you stay."

"Thank you," Denny said. "You're very kind. But... my beliefs don't allow it."

"That is as I expected. Now, to this morning's real business. We are having a meeting with our sponsors and I wish you to accompany me and advise me personally."

"Of course," Woolfe said. "What stage have negotiations reached?"

"We have agreed in principal to carry the colours of BSA Motorcycles." Goliath grinned broadly. "No payment has been discussed yet."

"I see."

"You will not let them cheat me, Ernie."

"I don't think they'd dare try."

The sponsorship negotiations went well and both sides seemed happy with the deal that was struck. Denny was amazed at the amount of money that BSA were prepared to pay the Philistines for wearing their logo on their chests. After all, they were going to lose. Even after Woolfe explained about the potential brand exposure, Denny found it hard to see why anyone would want to associate with a bunch of losers.

"Maybe if the outcome was ever in doubt," Woolfe said, "sponsoring the losers might have negative connotations. But this is history. Anyway, it's Goliath that does the losing and carries the can for it."

*

Most of the time their job was merely to keep Goliath happy. Keeping him out of fights was also important as they quickly discovered. As the champion of his people he was revered and respected, but having won his title by defeating the best his people had to offer, proving himself was also part of the job. The last thing the BBC needed was for one of the stars of the show to pick up an injury, or worse, get himself killed.

It had always been difficult for Denny to understand, as it was for most laymen, the flexible nature of time. Just because Goliath had been champion of the Philistines as a matter of history in Denny's home time, didn't mean he would necessarily survive to fight David in this particular segment of time. It was unlikely that any change would occur but always possible, as the television crew had affected the current reality by their very presence. But if it was flexible, time also tended to bend back into the shape it had always held, pulled onto the required track by the weight of history that would follow.

Goliath was not a particularly difficult assignment. He was friendly, wanted to be liked and was always keen to please the television crew. Unlike many of his countrymen, and warriors down the ages, he was even co-operative with the make-up team. When the time came for a make-up test he was like a lamb. He was even gracious about the mess they made of his precious tent.

The make-up artist who had been assigned to Goliath was a woman in late middle age called Miriam. There was still evidence that she had been a looker in her day but breasts, belly and bottom had all sagged and her attire had not taken that into account. She wore a brightly flowered, halter top, cut away from her meaty shoulders. Probably a one-piece, Denny decided, like a bathing costume. A pair of stretch denim jeans did nothing for her figure either. Her hair was definitely her best feature; there was oceans of it, nut brown with tiny flecks of grey which almost succeeded in looking like an effect her stylist had spent hours achieving.

At first Goliath ignored her, as he did all women. He sat obediently in Miriam's special chair as though pancake was second nature to him. Denny and Woolfe couldn't help but be amused as they watched her fussing over the enormous champion. She cranked the chair down to its lowest level and still needed a stool to stand on part of the time. "My, but you're a big one," she said at regular intervals.

Her team washed and conditioned Goliath's hair and beard, shaved his cheeks and neck, plucked his eyebrows and whitened his teeth. Miriam lightened his skin tone a couple of degrees. "Better contrast with hair and beard," she explained.

She stood him up and made him turn in a circle. "What about costume?" she asked.

"That is none of your concern," Goliath said dismissively.

"Short sleeves, bare chest, bare legs," she said. "Any of those could present a problem to the cameraman."

flip onto its back. Clouds of dust enveloped the cab. Blinded, Denny braced himself for the inevitable impact. It never came. Inertia and entropy won the day. The protesting vehicle juddered to a halt.

For several minutes Denny sat very still. He mumbled thanks to whatever gods were watching over him. When the dust settled he saw the backs of the retreating Philistines, their spirits broken by the death of their champion. He turned in his seat, wincing at the jagged pain in his side where the steering wheel had broken a couple of ribs. The OB unit was in total disarray. Even at this distance he could make out Cobham interrogating the camera operators. As usual, his only concern was to confirm that they had got the shot.

Closer, in the foreground, lay the unmistakable bulk of the big fellow. His armour was battered and crushed, his magnificent physique now robbed of all life and vitality. Denny rose painfully from his seat, eased himself slowly down the steps and out onto the sand. He could not bring himself to approach the broken figure of Goliath. He did not want to talk to Cobham's minions.

Denny walked away from the bus, into the desert. He needed to be alone with his grief. He needed to mourn his friends. No, not friends, they were more than that. They had given form to a new myth.

To Be A King

It would take more than bouncing along a pitted back road to keep Jesse awake. They were near the end of a two day run and his brother was at the wheel for the final leg. His lids closed heavily and his head lolled onto his chest. A faint nasal whine was drowned by the strident chug of the eighteen wheeler's engine. Ronnie contentedly wrestled the bucking steering wheel. The white line split the centre of the cab. Blacktop melted in the hot afternoon sun.

On a short straight the driver leant forward and switched on the radio. A country song was playing. Something about an unhappy love affair and an unfaithful wife. Ronnie could imagine the singer, tall and broad shouldered, a vast cowboy hat shading his face, a fancy embroidered shirt flashing rhinestones, fresh blue jeans tucked into hand-tooled boots. He glanced down at his own sweaty attire: a stained tee-shirt made to look a size too small by bulging work-hardened biceps, a pair of Levi's from which all colour had long ago bled at thigh and knee, the air of honest poverty accentuated by boots with one sole parting company from the scuffed uppers.

Jesse, though they were equal partners, was the brains of the operation. It was necessary for him to spend a little extra on his clothes. He had to look right for negotiating contracts and such like. Ronnie knew that, but he couldn't help envy his brother the shiny clasp of his bootlace tie or his sharp corduroy jacket. One day, when they were rich, Ronnie would wear flashy clothes. Even to church. He would stand up proud in the front of the choir and sing his solo in a white suit. With maybe some braiding on the sleeves and gold piping at the collar. He would never wear anything but silk shirts. He wondered if Reverend Hawkins would allow him to wear shades to service. That would be fine. How the girls would sigh over him. He could almost feel their eyes caressing him. He'd pick one out of the congregation and sing special for her, stare at her throughout the hymn so she would know.

The country songs came hard and mournful on the radio. Ronnie twirled the dial until he hit a black-music station. As long as Jessie was asleep he could listen to whatever he wanted. Sam Cooke was playing. Man, what a voice that dude had. Ronnie's hands tapped out time to the R'n'B that mirrored the speeding rhythm of the truck's spinning wheels, as he eased down the power. The next track was even faster. The needle on the speedometer crept up to sixty-five, the engine humming sweetly in counterpoint.

The truck was only three years old, and the newest the brothers had owned. Jessie was determined it would last them another two years. The way he had things planned they should be able to buy a brand new truck by then. Maybe even keep the old one, run two trucks. Ronnie was glad he had his brother to look after him. Planning was never one of his strong points. For twins, they sure had little enough in common.

The doctor said they were identical twins, though anyone with half an eye would dispute it. Jessie was small, bird-like and pale, his brother husky and darkly handsome. All through their childhood he had been sickly. But he was sharp as a tack when it came to figuring. All the years he spent in bed with nothing for company but some battered old book loaned by kindly neighbours, gave him lots of practice at thinking and planning. He had spent his whole childhood at it.

He planned how they would get themselves out of the poverty trap they were born into. Jesse was not contented to be poor white trash like his parents. He had ambition. He wanted to be a businessman. From the time he was ten years old he had told Ronnie how it was going to work. 'You'll do what you're good at and I'll do what I'm good at.' It was his way of saying you be the muscle and I'll be the brains. Ronnie understood that, and he didn't mind. He didn't see it as a slight. There was nothing wrong in admitting what was plain for all to see. Without Jesse to guide him and look after him, Ronnie would be in a sorry state.

The only time in his entire life he had been without Jesse, he got himself into trouble. Nearly got his fool self killed.

Jesse was in the hospital; something to do with liver problems. It was serious enough that he had been transferred up to Memphis. Ronnie borrowed his father's battered pickup and visited him. Afterwards, instead of going straight home, Ronnie went for a couple of drinks, played some pool, got to talking with the band who were playing in the bar. They seemed like real nice fellas and liked him well enough too. So when he told them he liked to sing they invited him to join them on stage during the second set. He sang a couple of gospel numbers with them and they persuaded him to try a couple bluesy things by Big Bill Broonzy. It felt good. The crowd liked it and the band thought he was pretty good.

'Me and my brother, Jesse, sing a bit,' he told them afterwards. 'We won a couple of talent contests. Of course, Jesse's the one with the talent. He plays the piano real nice and the way he weaves his voice in and out of mine makes it sound like there's four of us on stage. He sure is clever, my brother. I reckon, if he wanted to, Jesse could be just about anything he wanted to be. He could even be a professional musician. If he took the time out to practice. If he didn't have to spend so much time lookin' out for me.'

The band reckoned Ronnie could be a professional singer. All he had to do was tag along with them. They needed a singer. Three of them shared lead vocals, 'but ain't one of us worth a damn,' the drummer said. 'Why don't you come with us? We're going to Greenville tomorrow. Jackson on Saturday. You could be fronting the band in a couple weeks. What do you say?'

Ronnie said he had commitments.

The drummer reminded him about how Jesse could be anything, if he didn't have to look out for Ronnie. Then he bought him a few more beers.

Six weeks later Jesse came and collected him from hospital in Pensacola, Florida. He sang in the band for five weeks. The van they were travelling in blew a tyre and ran off the road. The drummer was killed. Ronnie would have a limp for the rest of his life to remind him of his short career in showbusiness. Him and Jesse never talked about it much. Jesse just included his brother in all his plans, like he always had before, like nothing had happened. The one time they did get into it, late at night, with a good few beers on board, Ronnie admitted it was the best five weeks of his life. Jesse cried. Ronnie realised how insensitive he had been. There was no taking it back, but it was never discussed again.

Ronnie glanced over at his brother, sleeping in the cab. Despite the physical disadvantages he had been born with, Jesse would never willingly let his brother do more than his share of the work. He had a weird formula for equating physical effort to brain work. But it always entailed Jesse pushing himself to his limits on the manual aspects of the job. Ronnie did what he could to ease his brother's burden, but Jesse had a sense of responsibility that he could not easily fathom. He was only happy when he matched his bigger, stronger twin in physical effort and achievement. Today he had worn himself out, taking a final spell behind the wheel that was really unnecessary.

Ronnie checked his watch. They would be home for lunch. He could almost taste his favourite burgers, made as only his mother could. Then he could get his head down for three or four hours in preparation for the contest later in the evening. Jesse stirred and his head slipped off the seat to knock against the window. He jerked awake, blinking in the glare of the spring sunlight like some nocturnal animal. He got his bearings rapidly then looked accusingly at the radio.

"You know how I feel about that stuff," he said, tuning out the black station in favour of Hank Williams. "Maybe I'll be able to get back to sleep now." He peered out the window, watching for a road sign. The first one along told him they were less than thirty miles from home. "Hell, I've only lost forty-five minutes shut-eye." His eye caught the speedometer. "More like thirty the way you're driving."

Ronnie accepted the criticism and eased his foot off the gas. He didn't want to get Jesse annoyed at him before the contest. This contest especially. Jesse had been known to purposefully perform below his best in order to punish Ronnie. Sometimes just to frustrate him. There had been times Ronnie had even thought of performing solo, just him and his guitar and his voice, but he knew that sort of thinking was futile. He didn't possess the classic crooner's voice he would need to survive on his own. And his piano playing was hardly up to the standard needed for a solo performer.

For tonight's show he needed his brother more than Jesse needed him. As usual. But especially tonight. The prize, apart from the usual cash, was something very special. The winners of tonight's contest got a once-in-a-lifetime opportunity to meet The King. Which would mean less than nothing to Jesse. But for Ronnie, it would be the high point of his life. For Rae-Anne also. He could imagine her fainting into his arms as The King walked into the room. He could imagine her saying yes if he asked her to marry him. She couldn't refuse him this time, especially after he won her the chance to meet The King.

Ronnie stood in the wings at the side of the stage, watching a four-piece band banging out a rock 'n' roll number. They probably thought they would have an advantage, seeing as the king of rock 'n' roll, Carl Perkins himself, was guest of honour at the contest. One of the judges had even been in his band – before he became a star. Of course, as everyone knew, Jimmy Duke was a good old country boy who had got out of the band when the black rhythms appeared. Smart move, Jesse had said at the time. He still stood by that opinion. Jimmy did a lot of work down at the Sun studios as a session player. That was good, steady work. Who knew how long rock 'n' roll would last. As long as the hula hoop? Who could tell. One thing was certain though, Jimmy would do the rock 'n' rollers no favours.

Rae-Anne squeezed Ronnie's hand. He was jigging nervously from one foot to the other. Perhaps he was enjoying his rivals' music. Rae-Anne wished Ronnie would give his brother the elbow and play the songs that were in his heart rather than the cabaret-fodder Jesse forced on him. That Jesse was a real control freak. He had even insisted, at the age of fifteen, on changing his brother's name before he would agree to play on stage with him. She remembered sitting on the back porch of their parents' home, Jesse swinging on his daddy's rocking chair, his jealous eyes watching his beautiful brother, younger by a matter of minutes. Even then Ronnie was good-looking enough to make a girl weep, with his sensuous mouth and piercing eyes and thick dark hair. Now with his hard trucker's body he really was a prime specimen. If only he could be given the confidence to recognise his own gifts. Like his God-given voice. If only he didn't listen to that insidiously poisonous little viper of a brother of his.

She remembered the way Jesse had embarrassed his brother into adopting his middle name. 'What sort 'a half-assed baby name is that anyway? Elvis. That's a name for momma's ittle bitty baby boy, not a full-growed man. Now Aaron, that's a man's name. We're going to call you Aaron from now on. That's a name for a man. A name for a man who's going to be famous. Aaron Presley. Ain't that got a ring to it.'

But he couldn't even leave it at Aaron. Even that he had to take away, as if by completely re-naming his brother he had taken possession of him. In a way he had been right. Elvis was a name for Momma's boy. Aaron was a name for a strong, independent man. Which was why Jesse changed it. Turned Aaron into Ronnie. And Ronnie into Jesse's boy.

Ronnie was sulking, which was potentially disastrous to the Presley brothers' chances of winning the contest. Rae-Anne peeped around the curtain at the side of the stage to stare longingly at The King. He was too close for her to miss this chance. It might never come again. The rumour mill said he was going into the army. She would have to snap Ronnie out of his present humour, though.

Of course it was her fault for mentioning any lack of respect for Jesse. She knew she should apologise, claim she said it because she was feeling mean. Time of the month. He would smile and pat her hand and everything would be all right.

But it wouldn't be. She loved Ronnie and he loved her but she would never marry him until he discovered some backbone, cut Jesse loose. She needed a sign. Ronnie knew it. She told him the last time he proposed. She tugged at his sleeve. He looked down at her, feigning annoyance but all she could see was adoration. She knew she would be good for Ronnie, as long as she was allowed to be. That meant no Jesse.

"Winning won't do it," she said.

Ronnie's brows knit in puzzlement.

"Getting me in to meet The King ain't no kinda sign."

The rock 'n' roll band finished their set to decent applause. There was a female country singer whose prime asset appeared to be legs that just wouldn't stop and a willingness to flash them throughout her performance. Fifteen minutes before they went on. Ronnie needed to see his brother. He would probably be in the dressing room they shared with the other acts. At least the males. The country singer with the legs had a room to herself. It was little bigger than a broom closet but it was all hers. Which had rightly pissed Jesse off.

As he expected Ronnie found his brother relaxing in the dressing room. He was talking to an older man and drinking from a hip flask. When Jesse saw him, he waved Ronnie over. "This is my brother, Ronnie. Ronnie, meet Mr Parker."

Ronnie nodded hello and shook hands.

"Mr Parker caught us down Tuscaloosa last month. Liked what he heard." Jesse screwed the top back on the hip flask and returned it to Parker. "Mr Parker's just leaving. Sorry for wasting your time, but you can hear it from the horse's mouth now. Ain't that right, Ronnie?"

Ronnie looked at Mr Parker whose eyes were locked with Jesse's.

"I was telling him about our plans. Our trucking company. About how we wasn't going to give that up for no half-assed promise from no two-bit hustler."

If there was one thing Jesse knew, it was hustlers. He could spot a scam a mile off, given his own liberal attitude to the truth where business was involved. If Jesse said Parker was a two-bit hustler that was good enough for Ronnie.

"You tell Mr Parker he ain't going to break up the Presley Brothers, Ronnie."

"He ain't heard the deal yet," Parker said.

"He don't need to hear the deal, do you, Ronnie?"

"No." Mr Parker was too much like Jesse for Ronnie's liking. One Jesse was hard enough for him to deal with. If there was two of him, hell, he wouldn't be able to pee without asking permission. Which Rae-Anne thought was the case already. And maybe she was right.

"I'd like to hear him say it after he heard the deal," Parker said.

"Sure." Jesse began nonchalantly rolling himself a cigarette. "Ronnie, Mr Parker here wants to sign you up. He wants to manage your career."

"Career?"

"You're a great singer, kid," Parker said. "I can make you a star. Even with the gimp. Look at Gene Vincent. All we need's a romantic story line to explain it. Like you was a…"

"No," Ronnie said. Parker wasn't even his manager yet and already he was re-inventing Ronnie. Maybe even inventing a brand new persona, someone or something Ronnie had never been. That would be the star, not Ronnie Presley. Or Aaron, or whoever he really was. The only one who had never wanted to change him was Rae-Anne. She was the only one who wanted him to be who he really was.

The door to the dressing room banged open and a stage hand drowned out Mr Parker's argument. "Presleys in two minutes."

Ronnie grabbed his guitar and Jesse smoothed his oiled black hair. They reached the stage as the country singer did a final twirl, showing her panties to Carl Perkins, and flounced off-stage to enthusiastic clapping and a wall of wolf-whistles.

Ronnie limped to centre stage as Jessie slipped behind the piano. He adjusted the mic stand, making it a good foot higher. The crowd were taking a long time to settle. He played a chord and Jesse responded in kind. He wished they had a drummer. A good drum roll would catch their attention. He thought about how their opening song would sound with drums to counterpoint the opening guitar chords. It was probably cheeky of them to choose The King's own *Blue Suede Shoes* to open with, but even Jesse could see the sense in it.

As the audience settled, Ronnie felt a shiver run through him. It was as though he had arrived at an important moment in his life and he could feel its significance even while it was happening. Tonight was going to be a turning point for him. Tonight there was someone watching him who could change his life. If he could grasp the moment.

He felt the power that knowing brought him. He stepped up close to the microphone and prised it out of its cradle. He made eye contact with The King and nodded at him as though they were old friends. Then he turned to the wings and looked into Rae-Anne's anxious face. "Good evening folks," he said, "my name is Elvis Presley." Rae-Anne's mouth opened in surprise, then her face flowered in the widest grin he could imagine. He turned back to the audience. Now was his moment.

The Pope, Sonny Liston and Me

They called him Wild Bill in the seminary. Somehow it always seemed appropriate. And the name stuck amongst family and friends. My father reckoned had he not risen through the hierarchy so rapidly he would have ended up in jail or burned at the stake. I never noticed that side of his character when I was a child; he was just my smiling Uncle Bill. I loved him, loved being in his company and looked forward to visiting him at any opportunity. Now that I'm an adult, a summons to Tara will always cause a slight tremor of apprehension. And of course, when The Pope calls, even his favourite nephew cannot refuse.

I tried to imagine what the old hill fort had looked like before the papacy moved in as I walked through the ringing corridors leading to Uncle Bill's private chambers. But it was just too ornate, too civilized, for the pre-Christian past to push through. The truth was there had probably been nothing but a hole in the ground back in the eighth century. Nobody had been too worried about ancient Irish history back then.

Even though I had been a regular visitor for a dozen years, protocol demanded that I be escorted by one of the Swiss Guards. Although he looked splendid in his formal dress green uniform I kind of missed the traditional garb Uncle Bill had abolished on his accession. His modernisation of the papacy had been almost universally unpopular but a decade later even his most ardent detractors had admitted that it had been good for the Church; particularly its image amongst the youth. For the past eight years, vocations had risen every year in every order in every country. It helped that Uncle Bill – Pius the XXI as I should more correctly call him – was the youngest pope since the sack of the Vatican. And that he was media friendly.

Not everything was sweetness and light however. Like any public figure, infallible or not, he had his failings. The worst of them was the one he shared with the Queen of England: he liked a flutter. With the Queen it was strictly the gee-gees but with Bill it was just about anything. I know it was one of the reasons we got on so well. As the manager of the World Heavyweight Boxing Champion, Alyoisus 'Chopper' O'Toole, I can get him tickets for any fight anywhere. His position as head of the Catholic Church probably means he doesn't really need that facility, but I can also get him backstage at title fights. He loves to drop in on the champ, and his opponent, all very informally, before a bout and hand out a blessing. Though on a couple of occasions his wicked sense of humour has got the better of him; he gave a Russian no-hoper the last rights and asked some short-ass who styled himself Iron Mike if he could use a quick exorcism.

Maybe it's something uncles have in common, but Bill always seemed to think my powers were limitless. In the early days I gave him a few tips and every time I got it wrong he seemed utterly astounded. Even when he lost big time on a fight, he would spend more time making excuses for me than worrying over the loss, which was never insubstantial. And once I realised what was going on I began making excuses as to why I couldn't be of help. Though after I began managing 'Chopper' the requests from Bill for tips on other fights dried up as he began to put his money firmly behind my fighter.

A door opened in front of me and I brushed past the Swiss Guard with a murmur of thanks. He snapped a crisp salute and closed the door with an almost imperceptible click. Uncle Bill bustled out from behind his enormous oak desk, threw his arms wide and pulled me into an effusive embrace as I ducked down into his grasp. What is it about world leaders and short stature? I won't attempt to compare Bill in any substantial way with Hitler, Mussolini and Napoleon, except that he is as short as any of them, and as bald as the Italian. You would think a man with his wealth and connections could get a decent wig, but the thing he wears looks for all the world like a shaggy rodent that lost an argument with a road roller.

"Jeff, my boy, how the hell are you?"

"Good thanks, Bill. And you? And Aunt Margaret?"

"Well, both well." He led me to the comfy chairs in his private nook at the back of the office and poured a couple of whiskies. I wasn't a great spirits drinker but he was a difficult man to oppose in even the most trivial things. "I'll get straight to the point, Jeff. I've got a meeting in about ten minutes. Bloody Canterbury and his ecumenical clap-trap. The Muslims have the right idea. I wish we had something like a jihad we could declare." He got a faraway look in his eyes, sipping thoughtfully at his whiskey. "A crusade against the Black Prods, what do you think, Jeff?" Then he giggled and plopped himself into his worn armchair. "No point in beating about the bush, I'm in the ka-ka. Up to my bloody neck in it, to be frank. Or Pius. Or whatever the hell it is I'm supposed to be." He laughed to himself again which was my cue to join in. "So to make a long story short, I find myself in dire need of some cash."

"Well, Bill, you know that whatever is mine is yours but what with the divorce and everything I'm a bit short myself and…"

He held his hands up for me to stop, most likely before I embarrassed myself. "I need a substantial amount. Five, six million or thereabouts."

"Whereabouts exactly?"

"Seven point nine million pounds sterling."

"Can I ask what you want to spend it on?"

"Already spent unfortunately. So I need to put it back before the books are audited."

"Put it back?"

"Petty cash. Well, it's from a discretionary account. If I, as pope, need money in a hurry without paperwork and bureaucracy I just drop a word to my bank manager."

"Very friendly manager."

"I'm not without influence with Banco Ambrosiano."

The mere thought of Banco Ambrosiano sent an uncomfortable shiver down my spine. Nobody messed with those guys. It was rumoured that one pope who crossed them died of unnatural causes in his sleep. And there was a French prime minister who came to a sudden and unexpected end while skiing in Austria. The police never did discover why he had been skiing in his pyjamas. This was out of my league in every way I could imagine. But Bill was my favourite uncle so I asked, "What can I do?"

"Chopper fights in six weeks. I need him to take a dive."

"What?" It was a severely inadequate response but all my brain and mouth were capable of managing in unison at that precise moment.

"Chopper is unbeatable. No bookie in the world is going to take a bet on him. But bets against him...?"

"Do people bet against him still?"

"It's like the Grand National. The grannies like a little bet on an outsider."

"Even the thought of asking Chopper to throw a fight is... is..."

"There's no asking, Jeff. You've got to tell him. I can't afford any bloody fannying about."

"Wait a minute. Slow down." I knocked back my whiskey to see if that would help. It sometimes did in the movies. But this was not the movies. When my coughing fit abated, I wiped the tears from my eyes and cleared my throat.

"Look, Jeff, I know it's a lot to ask but this is a matter of life or death. Otherwise I wouldn't even dream of it."

"Wait a minute, Uncle Bill, give me a chance to get in a word edgeways. The fight's off. Bruno broke his hand in training yesterday."

"You can get a substitute."

I shook my head slowly. "Bruno was the last credible contender. You know that as well as I do. Nobody's lasted beyond the third round in five years. HBO offered less than five mill for the rights to this fight. And they told me straight, no more Ukrainian mystery men, no more rematches and no more cannon fodder. Which leaves me with precisely no-one to put up against him. Let's face it, Chopper is just too good."

Uncle Bill seemed to shrink inside his clothes, like a balloon with a slow puncture. His wig canted over his left ear. He looked pathetic rather than funny. I felt an overwhelming urge to put my arms around him, hug him to my chest as though I were the uncle and he a little boy with a grazed knee.

"What am I going to do, Jeff? I'm bollixed." His chin tipped upwards and he looked me straight in the eyes. "They'll kill me, you know. Without a second thought."

"You're the pope for God's sake. They'd never get away with it."

"It's not like they'd just send a couple of heavies up from Dublin. They wouldn't just march into Tara and put a bullet in my head. But I'd be just as dead if my plane crashed or some virulent strain of salmonella got into my communion wafer." He giggled. For a minute I thought he was losing it. But there was a twinkle in his eye. "How many popely ways are there to go? Booby-trapped hat? Maybe a terrible sedan-chair accident. Or a fall off the balcony in St Patrick's when I'm doing my New Year speech."

"Come on, Uncle Bill, no-one's going to knock over the pope."

"If I don't pay them what I owe, they will do just that." He grabbed me by the arm, his small, sharp fingers pinching into my flesh, his eyes boring into mine sparked with genuine fear. "Believe me, boy, they will."

I believed him. And of a sudden I shared his fear. It was not the first time the following words passed my lips nor, I felt sure, would it be the last. "What happened to the money?"

He smiled with heavy irony. "A sure thing, of course."

"But seven, nearly eight million on a sure thing?"

"Well, more than one. Though only one was truly a sure thing. But... I doubled up a couple of times. Good bets, mind you. At good odds."

"Jesus Christ, seven point nine million. How could you?"

"Don't you take the name of the Lord in vain in my house," he snapped.

"Sorry."

My uncle poured himself a drink and stared into it thoughtfully for a while. "You were my last hope, Jeff. You and O'Toole."

"Unless you can bring Rocky Marciano or Joe Louis back to life, Chopper won't be fighting again soon. At least, not in a fight you could get a bet down on."

I glanced at my uncle. He was staring at me with a strange look on his face. The strange look began to fade into a grin. "Not Marciano, not Louis. Punks the both of them. Shit, we match him with Liston."

"Sonny Liston? He was just an animal."

"Undefeated heavyweight champion of the world. Ruled the division for twelve years."

"He was a crook. The mob owned him."

"But have you seen the footage on him? He was awesome. The best. We show the second Patterson fight as publicity, you can make a fortune selling the rights. The fight of the century. The two best heavyweights in history going nose to nose. You can't lose."

"But Sonny Liston is dead. Died in the seventies. Murdered."

Uncle Bill put an arm around my shoulder. "I'm going to let you in on a little secret the Church has been holding back. It's called time travel."

Poor Uncle Bill. The pressure had finally got to him and there was a crack a mile wide right through the middle of his brain.

"We kinda suppressed it when it was discovered but I've been thinking about bringing it into the open for a while and this might just be the time."

It never ceased to amaze me how many inventors were good Catholics. If the rumours were true there were several inventions lying in the basement at Tara waiting for the time to be doctrinally right. But time travel? "Time travel? That ranks up there with perpetual motion and anti-gravity. It's impossible."

He grinned and shook his head. "Anti-gravity eh? Shows what you know."

"You're not trying to tell me…"

"I'm telling you nothing. Except about time travel. We've got it and I'm prepared to use it. It's perfect. I'm a well known sports fan. The fight could be shown as a harmless way to demonstrate the benefits of time travel."

I had a sinking feeling in my gut. I no longer feared that my uncle was a basket case, but there are worse things than insanity. Especially for nephews.

Everything happened quickly after that. The Pope issued a press release announcing the existence of time travel and his intention to mount a harmless demonstration, though no mention was made of Sonny Liston initially. As Chopper's last fight had been cancelled there was still a free date in the calendar at Wembley, so I was persuaded to take a provisional booking, even though there appeared to be some problem securing the services of Liston.

"Don't worry," Uncle Bill said. "It's a minor hitch."

When pressed he admitted that the original plan had been to kidnap the fighter. He had decided to make the snatch when Liston was in training for a fight so that he would be in good condition. A routine defence against a pumped-up light-heavy called Clay was picked. The only thing that was overlooked was Liston's ability to look after himself. Four Swiss Guards were despatched and four returned. Without Liston, but with a wonderful selection of bruises and fractures.

"We're taking a different tack this time."

Uncle Bill would say no more, but two days later I was introduced to the great Sonny Liston. For the first time in a long while I began to worry about my fighter. This guy just oozed menace. There was a look in his eye that said he could kill any man in the room with his bare hands. And he would enjoy it. Did I want Chopper O'Toole in the ring with this monster?

"I've told Mister Liston that you'll be providing him training facilities and tapes of all of O'Toole's fights for him to study," Uncle Bill said after we shook hands, "but he would like to interview his own trainers and corner men."

"Just to make sure everythin's on the level." He slapped me on the back, perhaps a little harder than was called for and grinned evilly. "This bum O'Toole's as good's Pius here claims I'm gonna need to be sure I'm taken care of good." He winked broadly at Uncle Bill.

A look passed between them and I knew there was something, no, a lot of somethings, I wasn't being told.

My meeting with *Mister* Liston was short and to the point. He told me what he wanted and Uncle Bill answered for me, assuring our challenger that all would be as he required. Afterwards I collared my uncle. "What's going on, Uncle Bill? There's something you're not telling me."

Now Uncle Bill is a good liar but I am probably the person he most cares for in the world and that makes it difficult for him to keep the truth from me. Of course since he became pope nobody expects him to lie and he can tell the most outrageous porkies without anyone batting an eyelid. So he doesn't have to work as hard at it as before and maybe he's losing his edge. But it was written all over his face in neon letters that he was being less than honest.

"You think O'Toole can take this arsehole?" Uncle Bill asked.

It would be close but… "Yes. I think he can."

"How sure are you?"

"It'll be a good fight. But we'll take him."

"You're not a hundred percent though."

"No. Not one hundred percent."

"Ninety?"

"Seventy-five. Maybe eighty."

Uncle Bill nodded slowly, frowning deeply. "Even eighty isn't enough. I need a sure thing."

Suddenly it dawned on me. Of course. He'd nobbled Liston. "How could you Uncle Bill?"

"How could I what?"

"Liston's going to take a dive. That's… that's…" Despicable was the word I was searching for but I never got to that page in my mental dictionary.

"I wish it was that simple."

Now I was totally confused. Was there more? What more could there be. I waited while Uncle Bill cleared his throat and rearranged himself inside his robes. He had never looked more like a guilty schoolboy.

"I don't know Liston. I can't trust him. All he talks about is proving how nobody can stand up to him. This guy's ego is the size of Trinity College. He wants to prove he's the best there ever was."

"He's a crook. Half his fights were fixed if the rumours are even slightly true."

"I had to make certain guarantees before he would agree to come."

I stared at my uncle. I could feel my lips tightening into a spinster's scowl. I had a feeling I knew what more there could be, and just how bad it could get.

"I need a sure thing."

I shook my head, unable to speak. How could he even ask me this.

"Please, Jeff, I'm begging you."

"You think Chopper hasn't got pride? You think I haven't?"

"It's your pride or my neck."

"Chopper would never throw a fight."

"He'll do anything you tell him, Jeff."

"I can't."

"You have to."

I held out for over an hour. In the end I knew Uncle Bill's tears were fake but that he would stoop so low in order to persuade me was enough. It was a matter of life and death. At least, Uncle Bill was convinced he would die. And he convinced me. And I would convince Chopper. I was not proud of myself. For a long time I could not face myself in the mirror. But I justified it and I would still go to heaven. After all, I was saving the life of the pope. God would have to be grateful, have to forgive me.

From the day I met Liston there were four weeks to the fight. Both participants were in camps in the Dublin Mountains not five miles apart. That was handy for the journalists. The fight had really caught the public's imagination. In polls of the best boxers in history Sonny Liston regularly came out in the top three. Plenty of respected opinion put him in top spot but O'Toole was the fighter who had everything. He was taller, heavier and had a longer reach than Liston. In twenty nine professional fights he had never been beaten and only three times had he even been taken the distance. Of course the pundits moaned about the lack of talent in the division but there were plenty of experts who reckoned the pool of talent was as strong as it had ever been, it was just that O'Toole was so far ahead of the pack. I tended to agree with them and I had been more excited by the prospect of matching him with Liston than I had liked to admit. Could my fighter prove he was the best ever? But now I would never know. Chopper O'Toole was going down in the fifth and Pope Pius XXI had secured odds of four to one against that eventuality. It was a good price. The best odds available were only seven to one and that was on Liston being dropped in the first.

Apart from looking myself in the eye I also found it next to impossible to face Chopper. My uncle was right, Chopper would take a fall if I asked him, but I couldn't ask him yet. He was too honest. Everybody would see it in him immediately. I was going to have to wait until the last minute. So I spent as much time away from camp as I could. I called it spying out the opposition but it was really just hiding from Chopper. It wasn't strictly kosher for me to spend time in Liston's camp but what was kosher about the fight anyway.

For two weeks I listened to Liston drone on incessantly about how he was going to 'murder the bum' and watched as he destroyed a succession of sparring partners with alarming ease. I watched him smile through the carnage – he was enjoying himself. He was having a ball. Like a rabbit caught in the glare of a car's headlights I sat and stared in awed fascination at the most brutal display of legal thuggery I had ever witnessed. Day after day he was going though four or five sparring partners, battering them until their senses left their bodies or until the punishment outweighed their pay packets. I was in awe of the man and his strength. Technically I've seen a lot better but apart from Chopper at his best I couldn't think of a single boxer I would want to back against this man.

Then the rumours started to seep out of the O'Toole camp. Chopper wasn't happy. He wasn't training properly. He was scared. Suddenly the odds on Liston shortened. Uncle Bill was smug about his odds. I needed to talk to my boy.

"Why didn't you tell me," Chopper said.

I tried pleading ignorance but I knew at once there was no point. "Tell you what?"

"The fix is in." Chopper was angry. For a moment I thought he was going to hit me. "I had a visit from… your connections. I'm going down in the fifth. Everyone knows it. Everyone except me."

I stood helplessly by and watched the heavyweight champion of the world cry his eyes out. "How could you do it to me, Jeff? I thought you were my friend. But you turn out to be a rat."

There was nothing I could say to him. Everything he thought about me was true. Rat was far too nice a word for me. I placed a hand lightly on his shoulder. "I'll make it up to you, Eugene. I'll take care of you."

He knocked my hand away. "I trusted you like a brother."

A brother, yeah. Caesere Borgia, maybe.

Fuelled by self-loathing I paid The Pope a visit. "Keep your goons away from O'Toole."

He looked genuinely surprised. "I sent no-one. Jesus H. Christ, why would I do something like that?"

He was telling the truth. And it was a good question, why would he?

60

Why would anybody?

It was a week until the fight and still Liston beat up sparring partners, as many as could be arranged. I sat at ringside and watched him. Two days before the fight my brain began working again. For the past four weeks I had been knocked off kilter, maybe that was why I hadn't noticed what was happening. Liston wasn't training at all. Sparring is all very good in its place, but there's more to training than that. Liston was entertaining himself. I needed to talk to my uncle again. Fast.

"How did you persuade Liston to take the fight? You told him it would be a fix, didn't you."

"No. Honest. He said he wouldn't come unless I would guarantee a fair fight."

"So how *did* you persuade him then?"

"Money of course."

"That's it?"

"One million pounds worth of gold."

"Why gold?"

"Our money's no good in his time. He wants to bring his purse back in gold."

"Okay. Makes sense. Not a lot of money though."

"It is in 1963."

"Of course."

"So anyway, I had to introduce him to a gentleman who deals in gold bullion."

"Why didn't you just give him the gold straight?"

"Liston trusts no-one. Said he had to turn the cash into gold himself."

"So when does he meet this guy?"

"They met already."

"You paid Liston in advance?"

"Bastard wouldn't come otherwise."

"How could you be such an eegit." The words were out before I realised. I had never in any way shown disrespect for my uncle and I didn't mean to now. Before he could say anything I apologised. He threw me a puzzled look.

"The gold dealer, give me his address." Uncle Bill opened his mouth to begin an interrogation. I held up my hand. "There's no time. The address. Please, Uncle Bill."

The dealer was in Dublin, a forty minute drive away. The business day would be finished by the time I got there and it would be tomorrow, the day of the fight, before I could get to him. Unless...

The popemobile is probably the fastest car on the road in Ireland. For security reasons of course. The fact that Pope Pius XXI fancies himself as a boy racer is beside the point. Uncle Bill jammed his foot to the floor and ignored every traffic signal on the way into Dublin. No policeman in his right mind is going to stop the pope in full flow. And the popemobile is well known on those roads; everybody with a strong survival instinct gives it right of way.

J. E. Harris himself was locking the front door as we pulled up outside his premises on Ormonde Quay. As I clambered from the car I called to him. "Mr Harris? Can I have a word?"

"We're closed," he said.

Uncle Bill stepped out of the driver's side. "I would consider it a personal favour if you would give my nephew five minutes of your time, Mr Harris."

Mr Harris re-opened the door to his shop and led me inside. Uncle Bill got back into his car. He had gathered during our drive from Tara that I wanted privacy. He deserved to be left in the dark to worry. I shouldn't have called him an eegit but that did not mean he hadn't acted like one.

"The gentleman my uncle introduced to you some weeks ago..."

"Mr Liston?"

"The very man. What arrangement did you come to?"

"That's confidential."

I turned and looked towards my uncle through the shop window. "I am not being melodramatic when I say that the life of that wonderful man out there may be at stake." I looked around as though checking to see if we were alone, then stepped close to Mr Harris and in a hushed voice said, "There's a plot."

Harris looked out at the popemobile's smoked windows then back to me. "Uh huh," he mumbled, then squared his shoulders and went into the back room. He brought back a ledger that he placed on a glass display case containing English Sovereigns. He nodded at the book. "I simply cannot break a client's trust."

I flicked through the book until I found the entry against Liston. "Eight million?" I exclaimed. I have never claimed to be psychic but in that moment I knew without doubt that Chopper O'Toole was going to win tomorrow's fight. In the first to be precise. By knockout. And a bet of one million pounds placed at seven to one plus the original stake would leave Mr Liston with exactly eight million pounds. It looked like Uncle Bill was up the creek without a paddle.

"Looks like I'm up shit creek without a paddle," he said when I told him the situation.

"How much can you raise? We can still get a bet down."

"I've borrowed every penny I could raise to bet on my sure thing. The cupboard is bare and I am a dead man." As we sat in the car with rush hour traffic streaming past us there was a sharp knock on the window from some uniformed moron. Uncle Bill opened his window half way.

"If you don't shift it I'm going to clamp you."

"Fuck off, I'm the pope," said Uncle Bill and closed his window. He turned in his seat to face me. "You got any cash?"

"You've already had every penny I own."

"Oh. Right. What about your mother?"

"Re-mortgaged her house because Desert Rose couldn't lose at Sandown Park last May, remember?"

He had the decency to blush at the reminder.

"May as well throw myself in the Liffey," he said.

I knew there was a shred of hope then. The tide was out. "Maybe I can call in a few favours, raise some cash," I said.

"Look, even if you were creditworthy, how are you going to raise the money and get the bets down in under twenty-four hours?"
I shrugged my shoulders.

"Anyway, you've got a fighter to take care of. And a fight to win." He smiled bravely and patted my shoulder. "Don't worry about me, I'm a survivor. And nobody's going to bump off the pope for Christ's sake."

The fight was as anti-climactic as a case of brewer's droop. Two minutes and nine seconds into the bout Chopper O'Toole swung over a right cross which seemed to catch Liston a glancing blow on the cheek.

Down he went as though his skeleton had been extracted. No-one looked more surprised than Eugene 'Chopper' O'Toole. Up until yesterday he was throwing the fight. The previous evening he had been assured by his manager, yours truly, that that would no longer be necessary. And today he had knocked out the best fighter from history with a bitch slap. All he could say in interviews after the match was, 'Don't ask me.' For weeks afterwards he could be seen walking around Dublin, shaking his head and muttering to himself. His retirement announcement came as a surprise to no-one.

The morning after the fight I rushed up to Tara. Even though Chopper's purse had been cut to a million because of the nature of the challenger and the fact that it had to be a non-title bout, I had money. The whole million. Chopper said it wasn't his because he didn't fight for it and he didn't want it. I was desperate enough to let him give it to me. He would change his mind in a few weeks and I would get it back to him but just then I needed the money to see if I could use it to buy my uncle some time.

It didn't surprise me that The Pope was unavailable. I said I would wait. Four hours later Uncle Bill appeared. He was flanked by a couple of heavies in tight mohair suits with bulges under the armpit and wearing shades even though it was raining. Uncle Bill looked calm and confident. Or possibly he was simply resigned to his fate. Were they just going to take him out into the gardens or onto the hill itself and put a bullet into the base of his neck? I couldn't just stand by and watch. I had to make an attempt to save him.

I broke away from the Swiss Guards who were standing idly by, keeping everyone except the killers away from the pope. Waving the cheque, I ran to my uncle. "Give them this. It's better than nothing. A gesture of good will."

"Gentlemen, this is my nephew, Jeff. He's a little confused at the moment."

"We can make a fight of it," I said. "You have security. We can hold out for weeks. Months."

A security van pulled into the drive and drove straight towards us. It was followed by a second van from a different company. The first van stopped and a man in a flat cap leaned out the window. "You Pius

XXI?" he said to my uncle. Uncle Bill nodded. "Sign here," the man said, thrusting a clipboard at him.

Uncle Bill signed and a pallet was unloaded from the van. One of the heavies in mohair lifted the tarpaulin covering the pallet. I caught a glimpse of gold bars.

"Is this Sonny Liston's gold?"

"Unfortunately Mr Liston had an urgent appointment and couldn't wait to accept delivery."

"Appointment?" I asked stupidly.

"With Mister Clay in 1963," he smiled. Turning to the men in mohair he said, "I trust you will return any excess there might be when this is turned into cash."

The heavies grunted and began to load the gold into the second security van without even unbuttoning their suits.

"But how..."

"Anything can be achieved with trust and the help of God, my son," he said in his best pious, preachy voice, as though he was uttering a soundbite for the tabloids. "And who is going to expect The Pope to rip them off?" He laughed. "Certainly not Mr Liston."

Trouble Ahead

July 5 200-

The *Hod Carrier* has been reviewed in *The New York Times*. Favourably. 'Most powerful debut novel of the decade.' That's going to look great on the cover.

September 9

Outline for my second book has been accepted by Left Hand Press. Sales of *Hod Carrier* are slow. How can this be with the reviews it's been getting. Talked with Gordie my agent this morning. He feels sure that he can interest one of the major publishing houses in a sequel to *Hod Carrier*. Doesn't he understand? I've done that novel. I've said all I have to say. I'm finished with the subject, the characters.

November 3

Judy thinks we should sell our apartment and move to the country. Maybe start a family. I've told her to wait until the money starts to roll in before she spends it.

The *New London Review* has accepted a short submission. £250 for two evenings work. Maybe I should concentrate on the shorter form. It certainly seems to pay better.

January 19

Gordie has swung a three book deal with MacmilliCent. LH Press are rush releasing *Thesaurus of the Heart*. I simply don't have enough time to write. How can I fulfil all my obligations?

The tender spot on the back of my neck is beginning to give me pain. I must make an appointment with the doctor.

February 26

I am a professional writer. Today I quit my job. I feel great. I wish Judy didn't look so worried. And she's letting it affect her in other little ways. The other night, she insisted that she heard someone moving about downstairs. Eventually I had to get out of bed and check. Of course there was no-one there. Yesterday, she arrived home with a revolver wrapped up in a sweater at the bottom of her shopping bag. It's an old Webley and Scott, a war souvenir of her father's. She's put it in the drawer of her bedside locker. It's loaded. She insists that she wouldn't be able to sleep without it for comfort. Nothing I said would make her change her mind. I wonder if a talk with a psychiatrist might not be in order.

March 9

Stand Magazine has accepted my second short story. Their rates aren't as good as the NLR, but still, it is my first sale as a professional. I have purchased a copy of The Writer's and Artist's Yearbook. Tomorrow I shall start writing at the shorter length in earnest. I didn't realise there were so many markets for fiction.

April 26

Another rejection slip. This was not part of the plan. Gordie has given me some American addresses, but the cost of postage to the States is horrific.

The lump on my neck seems to be getting smaller.

June 3

Thesaurus of the Heart launched to wider critical acclaim than *Hod Carrier*. Mike from LH Press is really enthusiastic about the initial orders from bookshops, in spite of the poor sales of its predecessor.

August 27

Hod Carrier remaindered.

More pain from the lump.

September 14

Finally managed to sell another short story. Thank God. The mortgage which I once considered modest has assumed the proportions of a small mountain on my monthly horizon.

September 21

The first book called for by my contract with MacmilliCent is due at the end of the month. I just can't seem to finish it. Who could work with this constant nagging pain from the back of the neck? I'll take the morning off tomorrow. Get Judy to make an appointment with the doctor for me.

October 1

I didn't realise that Gordie could be such a bastard. A one week extension – what good is that?

My God! I wasn't aware of how much this lump was growing. It must be the size of a grapefruit half.

October 9

Appointment with MacmilliCent this morning. Bump precluded the wearing of a collar and tie. I was forced to wear a roll neck sweater. Felt like such a slob.

November 2

Judy insists I see somebody about the growth on my neck. Hairs are beginning to appear on it. She refuses to sleep with me any more.

November 5

MacmilliCent have returned the first draft of *Worldwise*. Not commercial, they say. If they want commercial why don't they buy up Jackie Collins' back catalogue. I rang Gordie. He agrees with the publishers. What is this, some sort of conspiracy? I thought Gordie was supposed to be on my side.

This damned lump is making my life hell. I'm beginning to walk stooped over. It's still growing.

December 6

Posted *Worldwise* to Gordie. I trust it will appeal to the mass market now. I feel like I've been raped. I hope they're satisfied.

The physical act of writing has become difficult. I have to strain against the growth to keep my head upright. Most of the time away from the word-processor I spend looking at the floor. It's easier than fighting it.

December 9

Judy arranged for me to see the family doctor. Family doctor, that's a joke. I've never even met the man. He's her doctor. Women seem to need more regular medical attention than men.

I didn't go. Judy is really pissed off with me. She is going to make another appointment. Threats have been issued. If I don't go along this time, she'll leave me.

December 15

A really nasty fight today. I didn't go to the doctor again. Judy screamed at me. She slammed the door on her way out. At least she didn't pack a bag. She'll be back.

My wife doesn't understand me. Now there's a cliché I thought I'd never have to use.

December 16

I'm frightened.

Now that it's down on paper it seems so obvious. Why did I refuse to admit my fear? Mr Macho? I don't think so. Fear is such a normal, healthy reaction. I'm sorry that I denied it up until now. But I refuse to wallow in it. I will continue to work. I will beat this thing.

There's a guy I went to school with who's a doctor. Maybe it would be easier to deal with someone that I know.

Maybe not.

December 20

Judy came back. She packed a bag and left again. Happy Christmas. What am I going to do now? The bump has grown. I bear more than a passing resemblance to Quasimodo. People stare at me in the street. Without Judy I'm going to have to go out several times a week. I don't know if I can face this.

December 29

Gordie has been a brick. I don't know how I'd have got over the last few days without him. He's organised a woman to do my shopping, cooking and cleaning. How he came up with her at such short notice I'll never know. And at this time of year. Of course now he feels that he can press me harder. He wants me to remove almost everything of any merit from *Worldwise*. I refuse to gut it just to appeal to the lowest common denominator.

January 5

My charlady, Mrs Topes, reckons that the lump on my neck is becoming gnarled. It was quite smooth up until recently, except for the hair.

I must get back to my work. MacmilliCent are still unhappy with the novel. The changes have to be made. I need the next portion of my advance.

January 22

Mike from Left Hand returned my phone call. My royalty statement is on its way. There will be no cheque with it. Sales of Thesaurus are appalling.

February 19

The lump on the back of my neck has accelerated its growth. My chin is almost resting against my chest. It is extremely painful for me to work. Mrs Topes is convinced that the lump is developing features. Ears, nose, mouth, eyes. She reckons it's a head.

February 22

I think Mrs Topes is right. I'm afraid Mrs Topes is right. She helped me set up a series of mirrors through which I could view the back of my neck.

The lump has a face! The features are vestigial, but distinct.

February 27

Worldwise has gone to Gordie again. I fear that if it is not right this time, my publishers are going to throw their hat at it. Anyway, I doubt that I will be able to make any further changes. Writing has become physically difficult. The other head is growing again. My face is being crushed onto my chest. Even speech is difficult.

April 21

I refuse to give in to this monstrosity. It is amazing what you can achieve with a little persistence and a lot of determination. I have developed a whole new typing style. It is one-handed and consequently slow, but today I completed my first short story in three months. Maybe I can get back to *Worldwise* now. MacmilliCent were very understanding when I came clean about my illness. I may make the final changes at my leisure. There is no pressure from them at all.

The pressure is now coming from my bank manager. My income for the last three months was nil. I'm overdrawn by... a considerable amount. The mortgage on the apartment has not been paid since December.

The other head is no longer the biggest of my problems.

May 4

I have begun to experience blackouts.

June 6

Yesterday I woke up on the balcony. I was lying on my stomach, sunbathing I assume. Why would I lie on my stomach? It is extraordinarily uncomfortable, considering the angle at which my head currently sits. My nose and mouth were quite bruised.

June 8

This morning I thought I heard a chuckle coming from that thing behind me; the other head. It is now fully developed, though not quite equal in size to what I consider my real head. It is difficult to know how to think of this second head. I know nothing of it. I have only seen it on three occasions. But as it grows larger it has also been moving forward, forcing me, my head, my first head, further downwards.

Breathing is becoming difficult.

June 12

It's watching me.

July 15

The blackouts are becoming more frequent. My work is suffering. This morning I received a rejection for a story that I cannot even remember writing.

August 1

Mrs Topes claims that the head spoke to her while I was blacked out. I was sure that she would hand in her notice. She didn't. My charlady is certainly less fearful of the head than I.

August 6

I think I'll have a bash at *World Wise*. Maybe I can do something with it.

August 12

Madness beckons. But it is a particularly profitable form of madness. I received a cheque in the post from a magazine called *Undertow*. I've never heard of it. But payment on acceptance can't be bad. $400 for something entitled *Death Spoor*. I wonder what it's about?

August 15

World Wise is turning out better than I thought. Not a bad writer at all, really. Am I?

August 28

Another acceptance. This is encouraging. Adversity seems to have helped my art. I'm worried about the blackouts though. They are becoming more regular. I have been out for days at a stretch. The thing held a conversation with Mrs Topes during my last spell of unconsciousness. She reckons it is quite rational.

September 6

I am continually in pain. My head is squashed hard against my chest. My neck is strained as my chin has turned to the right.

The head leaned over and winked at me today. It tittered. I find it quite revolting. Mrs Topes appears to have become fond of it, claims it's got a nice personality.

September 20

Judy called to the apartment. She jumped when I addressed her and found it difficult to meet my eyes. She didn't stay long.

October 17

Posted *World Wise* to Gordy. Wait till he gets a load of the changes.

November 9

Gordy loved the rewrite. So did the boys at Mac's.

November 21

I am almost totally incapacitated by the constant agony. The head continues to grow and to move. I am afraid that by the time it is full size it will be sitting squarely athwart my shoulders. Is there anything that medical science can do for me?

December 4

The pain is lessening. My jawbone has become almost rubbery. I am amazed at how the human body copes with hardship.

December 11

Judy is back living with me. She has fired Mrs Topes.

The blackouts are severe now. I figure that I'm out well over fifty percent of the time. The last period I lost measured ninety-seven hours. I have begun to suspect that the other head runs my body at these times. Judy refuses to confirm or deny my suspicions. Why has she returned?

To all intents and purposes she dislikes me more now than when she initially left. I think that if I was capable of fending for myself I would throw her out.

December 16
Gordie called around today to discuss *Worldwise*. He was very evasive.

I have been reading back over this diary. I do not recognize some of the entries. Is it some form of split personality or – I can't even bring myself to write it down.

December 23
That other head is ruining my life. Gordy says I should get rid of it. *Creepy Worlds* accepted *The Soothsayer*. I'm really hot.

January 12
I can no longer speak. My face has become so slack that I cannot form my lips and tongue into the correct shapes. Judy refuses to read my notes. All is not well. I caught her kissing the other head. At least, that's what it looked like from my angle.

March 1
I have been invited to take part in *Start the Week* on BBC Radio 4 to discuss my meteoric rise in the world of horror/fantasy. Why did Gordie not explain my disability to them? It is embarrassing for me to have to write to the producer personally. I think I may have to let Gordie go.

April 28
Discovered myself in a doctor's surgery today. He told me my condition was operable.

August 17
Another doctor. This one ignored me entirely. Apart, that is, from blinding me with his pencil light.

August 19

I'm going to be rich. Who would have suspected that there was a first rate horror story hiding inside that piece of crap, *World Wise*?

August 21

I am going into hospital in three weeks. The surgeons assure me that I will be fully recovered in time for the launch of *World Wise*. I had better be. Gordy has committed me to touring the States for a round of book signings.

September 7

Hospitalization is imminent.

I'm afraid. I wish I knew what was happening while I'm blacked out. I have a terrible feeling that things are going wrong. The thing behind me is running my life now. I know it's stronger than me. I'm sure that it is me that will be excised in the forthcoming operation. It must seem logical to others. I can't speak. I'm seldom in control or even conscious. I can see how they assume the thing is more viable. I can see their reasoning, but I can't allow it to happen. This is my body, dammit. I won't let them take it away from me. But in the short period of control left to me, what can

September 19

I'm free. The thing is gone and I'm in full control. This is the first chance I've had to write. For some reason they wouldn't let me have my diary in the hospital. Evidence, the police said it was. And they've been asking me a lot of questions.

September 22

The police say I should get a lawyer. The charge will probably be murder.

Murder? How can it be murder? I explained to them what had happened. I asked the Detective Inspector in charge of the case, a very nice man, what he would have done in my circumstances. The thing, the other head – it makes me shudder even to think about it – was a growth, a parasite. I am the real me, the original owner of the body. It was just like lancing a boil. That's all. But they don't seem to understand. They say they have several statements to the effect that the thing was in almost complete control. It was more alive than I was, they're claiming.

Bullshit. It was always my body. That means the other head was also mine. They said it was an independent intelligence. So what? I blew its fucking brains out and I'm damn glad I did it. How can it be murder? The thing, the other head, belonged to this body.

My body is mine to do with as I wish.

September 24

Looks like they're dropping the murder charge. The Detective Inspector is pretty miffed. He seems to have taken a dislike to me. Perhaps he never liked me from the start. Maybe he was playing Mr Nice to see what he could get out of me. See if I would make a slip or something. I don't know? I told him the truth. I denied nothing. I hid nothing from him.

I wish Judy was here.

September 29

The critics have slated *World Wise*, but what do they know? My publishers love it, my agent loves it and the movie rights have already been optioned. I just wish I liked it.

October 4

I'm being charged tomorrow. The Detective Inspector says that I will be prosecuted to the full extent of the law. Bastard.

Suicide, he said, grinning all over his face, is still a crime in this country.

Camels

Marriage to Brett would be great, Joy was sure, if he would only stop trying to prove how much more he loved her than he had loved Sylvia. Perhaps he saw his break-up with Sylvia as a failure. Possibly he thought that showering his new fiancée with gifts and unceasing attention would show that their forthcoming union was a matter of choice. Not that anything Brett did was going to stop the gutter press printing their stories. Brett was public domain, due to a family fortune totalling in the tens of billions of dollars. He was always news, at the very least on the society pages, as was Sylvia. As was Joy. Now.

Brett Preston and Sylvia von Arnham had been the tabloid press's sweethearts, taking up where Charles and Di had left off three decades earlier. Sylvia was their twenty-first century edition of a fairytale princess. Fifth in line to the throne of Belgium, she was also a highly successful catwalk model. The camera loved her and, even before her affair with Brett, a day seldom passed without her picture appearing in a newspaper somewhere.

As one of the richest men in the world Brett Preston was also the subject of intense media coverage in his own right. If it wasn't a back page story on his latest bid to win the Americas Cup, it would be a piece inside on his company's latest acquisition or merely a photograph of him outside a club or a restaurant. Together with Sylvia, he was media dynamite.

Speculation about the break-up of their romance had been front page news for weeks. When it was finally confirmed the public had taken it like the death of a major figure. Gossip columnists wore black for days. Joy Gibson, pretty and popular as she was, could never truly replace Sylvia. After all, she was only an actress. And a TV actress at that. No-one in the tabloids cared how talented she was. Nor did they concern themselves with her charitable work.

She had caught Brett Preston on the rebound, in their estimation, and was not deserving of him. They felt Brett protested too much – professing the enormity of his love for her at every opportunity, telling anyone who would listen that she was his soul mate, a missing piece of his life that made him complete.

Joy didn't care what the media had to say about them. She loved Brett for himself, not any public persona he might wear. In her mind, there was no doubt that Brett returned her feelings, no question of getting him on the rebound. It did not matter to her in the slightest who had broken up with whom in her fiancée's last relationship. As she pulled the duvet over her head and rolled over to catch an extra five minutes sleep, the last thing on her mind was what the public thought of her engagement to Brett Preston.

A hand on her shoulder caressed her awake. At first the gentle rocking motion fitted into her dream of a railway journey, as she re-lived in her sleep the final excursion of the Orient Express. But the voice saying, 'Come on, love,' was definitely not that of a porter. She rolled onto her back and opened her eyes the merest fraction. Daylight streamed into the hotel bedroom through the open balcony doors. The faint sound of traffic wafted up from the streets of New York below.

Brett stood over her, a look of mild concern on his classically handsome face. Joy stretched languorously and smiled up at him. "Come on, love, we're late."

She propped herself onto one elbow and gave him an appraising glance. He was wearing a superbly cut business suit over a crisp white silk shirt and a hand painted tie by Harkus – the latest darling of the art world; a contemptible little man but admittedly, a genius. *We,* Joy thought, are not late for anything. Brett was never late. He had been born on time. As had his so-perfect former love, Sylvia. If he was so damn keen on getting to every appointment on the dot of the appointed hour, he should have taken her body clock into account and organised the meeting for the afternoon. It was bad enough getting up early when she was being paid for it. Joy was damned if she was going to do it without protest when she was on vacation.

"Please, Joy." Mild irritation furrowed his brow. "We're due there in just under an hour."

Joy stretched out a hand to the tray on the bedside table and helped herself to a croissant. Biting into the flaky, soft pastry she swung her legs onto the floor and walked naked into the bathroom. The hot needles of the steaming shower flushed away the last vestiges of sleep. She liked her life. She liked the privilege that went with being a star, even if a minor one. She enjoyed the comfort that came with being rich.

Rinsing shampoo out of her hair, Joy grinned to herself. She could hear Brett rattling through her wardrobe, attempting to save time by picking a selection of dresses from which she could choose an outfit. It amused her how vulnerable he was to the media's comparisons between Sylvia and herself. Arriving late to any function would have been unthinkable for the fairytale princess. Brett would be anticipating another black mark against them in the press. Another occasion on which Joy Gibson failed to measure up to the standard set by Sylvia von Arnhem; on which they, as a couple, failed to measure up.

Joy already had her attire chosen. It would take her ten minutes, tops, to dress and apply the tiny amount of make-up she used. Yves St Laurent were paying her a seven figure sum to promote their natural look. She thanked a generous God for the perfect skin which needed so little artificial assistance. The knowledge that Sylvia had never gone anywhere without spending an hour beforehand in front of the mirror smoothing out the imperfections, imagined or otherwise, gave Joy a pleasure she felt guilty indulging.

She swept out of the bathroom shaking the last drops of moisture from her short blonde hair. Brett hovered by the bed, where he had laid out the selection of dresses. She tossed him the hair dryer and shook her head, selecting a simple summer number in royal blue and slipping into it. The look on Brett's face when he realised she intended going without underwear almost caused her to laugh aloud with the sheer pleasure of being alive and able to do just about anything she wished. Joy crossed to him and took his face in her hands. "Don't ever change," she said. Turning to the mirror, she added, "We can make it on time if you dry my hair while I fix my face."

*

The Preston Industries annual stockholders' meeting at the Trump Tower II started dead on time. Joy's calculations of the timing were on the button. They were even early enough for the press to get all the photos they wanted without upsetting the schedule. The meeting ran for just over three hours. Joy placed herself anonymously amongst a cache of Mid-Western stockholders and used the time she remained trapped there to scan the news media on her notebook.

It was the usual doom and gloom. The US and Israel were still at loggerheads over the Libyan invasion. Martial law in Scotland was escalating the religious tensions; the UN had declared Glasgow an official environmental disaster area. France was still threatening to secede from the EU. Rumours that Sony's offer for Coca Cola would be accepted within the week were confirmed by a Coke vice-president. Joy turned to the trades. If they weren't careful the damn Koreans were going to own everything. She keyed for Daily Variety. Her agent had promised a half screen photo of her would appear this week.

By twelve-thirty the meeting was over and she was in the hotel lobby with Brett, pressing flesh with the real owners of the family business, or at least their proxies. Joy put her screen smile firmly in place and exchanged banalities with a procession of men who appeared to have in common a lack of hair, a lack of height and an excess of inches around the middle. Noticing that Brett was missing from the ordeal by handshake caused Joy mild annoyance. When he appeared from behind, excusing her from a knot of senior executives from the Chicago office, her attitude changed to profound gratitude.

He led her across the lobby to an alcove where a tall, lean man with a full head of hair waited for them. Whoever he was, he had nothing to do with the stockholders or their meeting, Joy was quite certain. His tanned weather-beaten complexion had not been gained sitting behind a desk for one; this was a man who spent the majority of his time exposed to the elements. For another, he was not wearing a tie.

She had noticed a sign as they entered the hotel earlier, proclaiming a meeting of the World Wildlife Fund in another conference room later in the day. She was prepared to bet that was why he was there.

Brett introduced the tanned man as Robin Shackleton. His handshake was firm and dry. His eyes met and held hers without a suggestion of the quick downward glance she usually experienced. Joy got the immediate impression that this was an unusually confident and competent man. The type who would succeed in whatever field he chose. She liked him at once.

"How would you like a week in Kenya?" Brett said.

"Sounds wonderful." Joy broke eye contact with Shackleton, surprised at how difficult it was. "What's the catch?"

"She can see right through me, Robin," Brett said. Then to Joy, "It's going to be the experience of a lifetime."

"I guarantee it," Shackleton said, in a voice that hardly rose above a whisper.

"No need for lavish claims. I've always wanted to go to Africa. Before it's turned into a parking lot."

"Then it's agreed."

"And the drawback?" Joy asked.

"We fly out tomorrow night," Shackleton said.

"Tomorrow? But we've got the premiere of Irving's new play."

"There'll be other premieres of other Irving plays. This is... This will be..."

Shackleton supplied the word Brett was groping for. "Unique," he said.

"So what is it that makes the trip unique?" Joy asked.

"A surprise," Brett said, a little boy's smile exploding across his face as though his whole body was hardly big enough to contain the enormity of his secret.

She knew there was nothing for it but to indulge him. His was a fault common amongst those raised in privileged surroundings – the expectation of such indulgence. No, she told herself, it was more than expectation. He could not conceive of a world in which his whims would not be instantly gratified. It was not his fault. His parents were to blame, leaving him, as they had, in the care of nannies and servants for his entire childhood. But she would be his salvation. And he was definitely worth saving. Despite his faults he was a nice guy. He craved love and had a lot of love to give. And, hell, he was exciting to be around. Things happened. Good things. She had thought her lifestyle before Brett had been exciting, but he was electric.

*

Nairobi airport was the busiest on the African continent. In the previous ten years it had tripled its capacity. A flight landed or took off every two seconds. The arrivals complex sprawled across an area of twenty-three hectares. Apart from the usual chainstores and concessions, Joy was surprised to see a bazaar. On the surface it appeared to be genuine, as though it had grown accidentally in unused space enclosed by the terminal's continual expansion.

But she had little chance to look around. Wherever Brett travelled, his itinerary was planned to the nth degree. A group of four men from a local Preston Industries subsidiary met them shortly after arrival. Even though supposedly on holiday, he could not help but utilise the trip as a business opportunity. The limousine which whisked them off to the Nairobi Hilton had the Preston logo displayed modestly on the front wing, just in front of the driver's door. Their escorts were deferential and smiled incessantly. Joy felt sure they would laugh easily if given the opportunity.

The unexpected, mobile meeting scenario was not a particular surprise to Joy. She had become used to them. They were part of the price of her forthcoming marriage into the Preston dynasty. She usually found that her use of a Viewman was appreciated by all concerned. It kept her from passing away from the boredom of intense executives spouting financial data and allowed them the luxury of ignoring the boss's fiancée.

A light touch on her arm told her that the limo had reached the hotel. Brett smiled into her eyes and whispered his promise to repay her understanding. He was quite graphic about the coinage he would use. If he had spoken aloud to a stranger he would have been arrested. She would be sure to hold him to his boast of repeated and extended bouts of lovemaking. There was something sexy about the feel of the African Continent. She was going to like it. Of that she was sure. And she would begin just as soon as Brett amply demonstrated that he was suitably impressed by the locals' stewardship of his company.

The meeting was interrupted terminally by the purring of Brett's phone. Whoever was calling had been given the emergency over-ride code, so it had to be important. He stood off to the side, nodding his head, saying very little. Joy watched him over the top of her Viewman shades.

After about four yesses and a long pause during which he stared out the window, Brett finally spoke a coherent sentence into the handset. "I don't like it, but okay." He listened for a moment then said, "You're trying to tell me that there are others in the group paying the same premium?" A longer pause while he listened intently, then, "As long as you guarantee me that final shot for Joy." A pause, then, "We'll be there."

He closed the phone and slipped it back into the breast pocket of his shirt. Turning back to the Preston executives he said, "Gentlemen, I must apologise. But I'm afraid it has become necessary to change my itinerary. Thank you for your hospitality, but unfortunately we must leave for the airport immediately. I've been very impressed with what I've seen so far. Perhaps you'd be good enough to put together a tape of your presentation for me to view when I get back to base."

The Kenyan executives made a great deal of fuss over showing their understanding of Mr Preston's need to change his plans. They would of course be honoured to make a tape for him and hopefully the next time he was in Nairobi he would set aside some time to visit the plant. It would be immensely motivational for the entire workforce.

Brett took Joy by the arm and rushed her from the suite. "What's happened?" she asked. "Wall Street crashed again?"

"Worse," he said. "Robin Shackleton has pulled the carpet out from under our safari."

"I don't believe it. He's cancelled? Just like that?"

"No. Not cancelled. He's changed venues." A Preston employee was waiting for them at the lift, holding the door open. Brett acknowledged him with a nod as they stepped past.

"I don't understand. Come on, Brett, you've been acting like the secret service ever since you first met Shackleton. Isn't it time you told me what's really going on?"

"It's exactly as I told you. The safari is special. Unique. But I don't want to spoil the surprise."

Joy was beginning to lose patience with him and his whole elaborate secret. "Can't we just cut Shackleton loose and stay here? Find another guide?"

Brett shook his head. "I told you, it's special. It's just for you. I want to show you just how much you mean to me."

"You've nothing to prove to me," Joy said.

The lift slid to a halt. The door chimed open. Brett's driver was waiting for them in the lobby. As they approached him, the uniformed man said, "Mr Shackleton telephoned me with the new schedule. We have twenty-nine minutes to get to the airport."

Brett quickened his pace, forcing Joy into something close to a trot. "Dammit," he said. "I knew I'd regret leaving the jet back in the States."

"You said Shackleton insisted."

"He did. Scheduled flights only."

"I don't see why you let this man dictate to you."

"No, he was right. He has his reasons."

Robin Shackleton met them at the airport personally. Joy didn't know why he bothered. His manner was brusque and he didn't bother apologising for the abrupt change of plans. He had seemed like such a perfect gentleman when they met in Chicago, now she was not so sure.

"What about our luggage?" she asked.

"All taken care of by my staff," Shackleton said.

"Where are we going?" Joy said.

Shackleton glanced a question at Brett who nodded almost imperceptibly. "Calcutta, then on to Urumqi," he said.

"Where is that?" Joy demanded. "I've never heard of it."

"China," Brett said.

"What's in this Urumqi place?"

Shackleton shook his head. "Nothing. It's the provincial capital. Closest international airport to where we want to go."

"Which is?"

"The Gashun Gobi."

"Is that Gobi, as in desert?" Joy said.

"Yes," Shackleton said, making no apologies for the harshness of their destination.

"We're going to the Gobi desert?"

"The Lop Nur game reserve."

She turned to Brett. "I don't believe this," she said. "I start out expecting a safari in Kenya and I end up in the fucking Gobi Desert? Which one of us is crazy? Please, reassure me that I'm wrong to think of a desert as a shitty place for a holiday." She gave him no time for reassurances of any kind, turning on her heel and marching across the concrete apron to the plane.

During the flight she treated Brett to several hours of silence. After dinner, despite the lack of privacy, she indulged in a loud, heated argument with him. At one point a petite Asian hostess approached them with a request to lower their voices in deference to the other passengers. For a short moment Brett and Joy were united, if only in their attack on the flight attendant. Consideration for others was the last thing on their minds at that moment and they were both quite eloquent in conveying that information to the woman.

The hostess smiled and nodded and attempted to argue. Joy was surprised at the range and vulgarity of the language she employed in communicating their desire to be left alone. When the hostess departed there was a moment of silence in which their falling out could have been patched over. Joy identified the moment correctly but was so furious at Brett that she ignored the opportunity and continued exactly where she had left off when the flight attendant interrupted her flow.

They continued to bicker through the change of planes at Calcutta, though the intensity and volume had abated. Less than an hour after the long flight into China began she took two sleeping pills washed down by a large Smirnoff and went to sleep.

The plane was circling Urumqi when Brett wakened her. She looked out the window at a sprawling, grimy city which appeared to have been trapped somewhere in the late twentieth century. Industrial chimneys pierced the sky everywhere, some of them still belching fossil fuel smoke. She treated Brett to a withering look and roundly ignored him until after they had disembarked.

Getting through customs and immigration proved anything but straightforward. Shackleton spent the guts of an hour arguing the toss with the airport officials, shuffling documentation back and forth. Joy estimated the size of the bribe which sorted out their problems to be in the area of a hundred thousand dollars. Obviously Shackleton had been prepared for such an eventuality. Although from where she sat she could not see fully into his attaché case, a considerable amount of currency still remained.

Once the formalities were out of the way Shackleton led his party back the way they had come. There were four others apart from Joy and Brett, none of whom seemed interested in social interaction of any description. One man was obviously Shackleton's assistant. Tall and rangy, he affected a bush jacket and army surplus trousers tucked into heavy boots. The others were all male and three were on the wrong side of middle age. If she had cared about their welfare in the slightest Joy would have worried about their ability to survive the depredations of the Gobi Desert. As things stood, she was prepared to enjoy their discomfort.

The party was led to a quiet hanger outside which stood a large, sleek helicopter. It looked as though it had borne military markings up until very recently. The low profile lines of its construction would render it virtually invisible to radar. Joy wondered why such technology was necessary. Perhaps it was the only charter available. They boarded in silence and lifted off without any pre-flight announcements from the crew.

One of the other customers, a large, bearded man with a loud voice, clambered out of his seat and made his way forward to the spot behind the pilots' seats where Shackleton sat. Beside the guide a metal case lay open, disclosing a computer terminal.

The large man leaned on the back of Shackleton's seat and looked down at the device. "What's happening?" he said. Although he probably thought of his tone as conversational, his voice boomed throughout the interior of the helicopter. Joy recognised the accent, she thought, as being from the Carolinas. He was the only other American. The other two were a slight gentleman with iron grey hair and an Oxbridge accent, and a startlingly handsome young man who had introduced himself with grave formality in the airport as Mr Bey, giving his nationality as Turkish.

Shackleton tapped out a command on the device's keyboard, then pointed to the screen. "The satellite shows the group to be moving south, Mr Hendy, towards the Desert of Lop."

"How close will the chopper take us?"

"Pilots estimate we'll be within a hundred miles of the group by dawn tomorrow. Maybe closer." He jerked a thumb towards the back of the craft. "There's two Land Rovers back there. We'll be in and out in two days, tops."

"What about patrols?"

"The nearest rangers are based at Tikar." He punched a further command into the device. The screen changed, displaying a map.

Shackleton pointed at a spot on the screen. "Here. There's a patrol in the general area at the moment but it should not interfere with our safari."

"And if they do?"

"They won't," Shackleton said, closing the lid on the case and on the conversation.

Joy could not make sense of the conversation. The patrols could only be wildlife rangers or the Chinese army. The only reason for avoiding either one would be a lack of official sanction for the safari. She turned to Brett, intending to get stuck into him again, this time maintaining the pressure until he put her fully in the picture. He was fast asleep. Waking him would be pointless. Tired and irritable, she would get nothing out of him.

She tried to sleep herself, but unsuccessfully. It was dark outside, there was nothing to see. She put on the Viewman shades and tuned in. A movie channel was running a twenty-four hour Johnny Depp retrospective. She wondered if there would ever be another actor like him. His funeral had been the biggest since Valentino's. There was a rumour that his head had been cryogenically frozen but considering the man's attitude to organ replacement in his latter years, it was doubtful he would be grateful for revival, no matter what advances had been made in geriatric medicine.

A spear of light announced the arrival of the dawn. Joy peeled off her shades and rubbed at tired eyes. Despite the vibration in the glass, she leant her head against the window. They were flying at a height of no more than one hundred feet. The ground which raced past was more desolate than she had imagined possible. Her mental picture had been of sand and oases; the reality was wind seared earth covered with a veneer of loose rocks. The sparse vegetation was stunted, withered and brown, clinging close to the inhospitable soil. The terrain looked cold and deadly.

The helicopter landed in the lee of a bare hill, with ridges pared to razor sharpness by wind-blown sand. Joy stepped from the craft, her back to the high ground. Before her stretched a bare, rippled landscape; horizon blending to infinite sky. Whatever they were looking for, she could not imagine it surviving in such a wasteland. Whatever lived here deserved to be allowed to cling to its tenuous existence. There would be no majesty in the beasts which claimed this barren tundra. There could be no romance in hunting them down.

"Ms Gibson." It was Shackleton.

She turned. The chopper was already rising into the air. As a passenger she had not noticed how little noise the vehicle made. Standing close as it took off, it was remarkable how silent it was in operation. Definitely military, she decided. The question was why such stealth technology was necessary for a safari, even if their papers were lacking a stamp or two. It had been a decade since there had been any travel restrictions in the Chinese interior worth talking about. Perhaps they were near a military zone.

"Please, Ms Gibson," Shackleton said. "We're ready to leave." He ushered her towards the first of the Land Rovers and took his place behind the wheel. Mr Bey was in the front passenger seat and Brett awaited her in the back. She climbed aboard, fastidiously leaving a wide gap between herself and her fiancée. Mr Bey half turned and smiled. His teeth were marvellously white, like finest mother of pearl. She smiled back, upping the wattage to ensure Brett noticed the by-play.

They drove for five hours, rocking across the trackless Gashun Gobi. Behind, the ceaseless winds erased any sign of their passing. They could have been alone in the world. Conversation was sporadic, strained and unfailingly polite. It soon became obvious they were heading for a line of low hills laid out like giant's fingers. The valleys between, Joy noticed as they drew close, boasted as much vegetation as they had seen at any stage since their arrival in the desert. Less than a mile short of the first valley, Shackleton stopped the Land Rover and got out. He went to the rear and pulled the metal case containing the satellite link onto the tailgate. Flipping it open, he keyed in the command codes and watched as the data downloaded. A broad grin spread across his face. "Got you," he said.

Joy climbed out of the vehicle. "Brett," she said, "Can I have a word with you?"

Brett slid across the back seat and exited by her door.

"I want to know what's going on. I want to know to the last detail and I want to know now." Her tone left no margin for argument.

Shackleton snapped the case closed and replaced it in the back of the vehicle. "Permit me to explain," he said, pulling a rectangular leather case out and slamming the back door.

Joy turned her gaze onto him. It was cold and uncharitable as the Gashun Gobi itself.

"I wanted to give you something that could never be replaced," Brett said. "An experience that could not be replicated or matched. I wanted to give you something so monumentally huge that you could never doubt what you mean to me."

Shackleton continued, "And I presented him with the perfect opportunity, the chance to give you something entirely unique." He pointed over her shoulder. "Look."

Joy turned, taking a line on his pointing finger. Had Shackleton not brought it to her attention, she would never have seen the animal which stood at the mouth of the nearest valley, so well did it blend into the dun background. She glanced at him quizzically.

"You see it?" he enquired.

"Is it a camel?"

"A Bactrian camel."

"Bactrian?" she said.

"Two humps."

"So?"

"You've seen camels before? In zoos?"

Joy nodded.

"Dromedaries. One hump."

"So?" she repeated, testily.

"The domestic Bactrian is extinct. That mutated bovine TB epidemic in '14. Only seven years ago the World Wildlife Organisation named the wild Bactrian camel the most endangered large mammal on the planet. There were seventy-one of them at that stage. Despite the best efforts of conservationists there are six left today."

Joy looked from Shackleton to Brett. Her fiancée smiled encouragingly. Shackleton unzipped the case he had taken from the Land Rover. Inside were two rifles. He took one from the case and, reaching into a separate compartment, produced a telescopic sight. "The circumstances of the Bactrian camel's present situation are indeed unique. Their survival, while unlikely, is still possible. They are healthy and fertile. Three females, two of which are pregnant, one male and two calves, one of each sex." He began attaching the sight to the rifle. "Our initial target was the final member of the species known as Barnette's Gazelle. But then this opportunity arose."

"I don't follow," Joy said.

"Your fiancée purchased from me the right to shoot the Barnette's Gazelle. The last member of its species. Something truly unique. Something that could never be replicated under any circumstances. It is the last Barnette's Gazelle. You would kill it, thus putting an end to an entire species." He beamed a huge grin at her.

For the first time in her life, Joy wished she were a man. She could think of nothing that would give her more pleasure than shoving that grin down Shackleton's throat. The turn the conversation had taken since her demand for information was totally unexpected. To give herself time to think she asked, "But why the camels?"

"This group is viable. That's the difference. If we ignore the gazelle it will eventually die. Old age. Run over by a lorry. Eaten by a predator. Shot by someone else. But whatever the case, the species is doomed, no matter what." The sight now in place, Shackleton leaned the rifle against the Land Rover and took hold of the second weapon, beginning to repeat the process almost as though it had therapeutic value. "But the camels could live. They could survive, with luck. Their extinction was not guaranteed." He paused for effect. "Until now."

Joy was having difficulty believing what she was hearing. The enormity of what Shackleton was discussing so calmly and proudly, the sheer abomination of it left her breathless and numbed. Her head felt as though a giant hand was squeezing it. At any moment her brain would shut down, her eyes would roll back into her head and she would disgrace herself by collapsing, full length, onto the desert floor.

She had always known that Brett was self-centred; what rich, only child was not? She had considered it a minor flaw in his character and one that a loving, attentive wife and the responsibilities of fatherhood could rectify. She had also recognised that he had little concern for the welfare of his workers, except in relation to how it affected productivity. That, she had assumed, was a result of the scale of the Preston Industries' worldwide operation. How could you care for individuals when there were 30,000 of them to think about? The answer she reached was, you couldn't. They became part of a machine; cogs in a vast wheel.

Now, all she knew for certain was that she had never really understood Brett. She had never allowed her picture of him to attain any depth. She had accepted his surface values, flaws and all, as his true self. But if he was capable of using his wealth to indulge in something so abhorrent, what else would he be capable of? Was he so insulated from the real world that he could fail to see how an act like this would disgust her? Or anyone?

Brett was shifting from foot to foot, like an eager child waiting for the approval of a parent. He really had no idea how she felt. Her eyes flickered onto Shackleton to be met by a flat, calculating stare. Their guide, the great white hunter, at least recognised that all might not be well. Quickly, she turned from them, shading her eyes from the glare of the sun, pretending to search for another sight of the camels.

Now the size of the bribe at the airport made sense. The need for a military helicopter was explained. The Chinese authorities had earned an appalling reputation with regard to wildlife conservation within their borders in the early years of the century, almost on a par with the predilection toward human rights violations of their predecessors. But for the past five years they had been making a concerted effort to stabilise their wildlife populations and conserve the species that were left; world opinion would not sit still for another panda debacle.

A crime against conservation on the scale Shackleton was planning would likely cause the Chinese authorities to respond with extreme prejudice. How would he react if she revealed her true feelings about him and his safari into hell? Could Brett protect her? Would they be prepared to take the risk of her blowing the whistle on them afterwards? She could not see Shackleton agreeing to abandon the safari just because it offended her. The profit motive was too great; his investment in the project was obviously substantial. If he was prepared to wipe out a species at the whim of a bunch of wealthy degenerates, what value did he put on human life?

"Are we driving in?" she asked, struggling to keep her voice even.

"We'll herd them all into the valley using the vehicles," Shackleton replied. "It's a dead end."

"In more ways than one," Brett laughed.

Acting on daytime soaps had not prepared her for a role like this. If she failed to be convincing the consequences were unthinkable.

Beginning with her breathing she began to construct a role. It was Shackleton who must be convinced and the man was no fool. It was probable he already suspected something was wrong. Her acting coach had always said that for TV, it was all in the eyes. Never was that more true than now.

Joy turned back to them, focusing entirely on the guide. Her breathing was short and fast, her eyes almost feverishly bright. She pitched her voice a half an octave above normal. She swallowed hard as though her mouth was dry; no acting needed there.

"Can I drive?" she said

The request threw Shackleton off balance. Of all the scenarios that had run through his head while he watched Joy scan the mouth of the valley, this one had been notably absent. "Have you ever driven a Land Rover?"

"A Jeep. But I'm sure they're similar." It was a lie. She had only driven a stick shift on a handful of occasions and off-road vehicles were a complete mystery to her. "Could you just run me through the transmission?"

Shackleton smiled, He had been worried about Joy's reaction. He had smelled trouble right from the moment she reacted negatively to their change of plan; when he realised Preston was keeping their ultimate goal a secret. But from the look of her, all he had to worry about was her wetting herself from the excitement of the chase. The upholstery was, after all, real leather.

"Come on." He led her to the Land Rover and sat her behind the wheel. She made him go over everything several times. When she was satisfied she knew how to operate the vehicle, Joy asked to be shown how to work the rifles, even though her father had taught her all about guns before her tenth birthday. She could not afford mistakes. Shackleton was only too pleased to oblige, taking pains to ensure she would be proficient.

Joy took her time with the rifle, checking the sights over and over again, fitting a magazine and levering a round into the chamber, ejecting it and refilling the clip. As she prepared to go through the operation for a third time, Shackleton left her to her own devices, strolling over to join the rest of the group who were chatting beside the second vehicle.

With great deliberation Joy snuggled the stock of the rifle into her shoulder. Leaning across the bonnet of the Land Rover she made herself comfortable. Carefully, she took aim, squeezing the trigger as her father had taught her all those years ago. The men scattered at the sound of the report. The other Land Rover jolted as one front tyre exploded. Slowly, with great precision, Joy took a bead on the second front tyre and blew it to shreds.

Everybody else huddled behind the stricken vehicle, screaming in fright or anger. Joy calmly climbed into the cab and drove into the nearby valley. At her approach the small group of camels bolted in panic. Keeping hard to the right hand slope, she gave the animals ample room to circle past her and escape from the dead-end. As they scattered past her she braked, swinging the Land Rover round behind them, driving them away from the potential trap. They looked underfed and mangy, but they were all there was in the world of Bactrian camels.

They had cost her a marriage at least, but given what she now knew about her fiancée, that was no loss. As she exited the valley she saw that Shackleton and his assistant were trotting towards her. Still a good hundred yards distant, they stopped, both dropping to one knee. She saw the rifles come up, watched them sight on her as she swerved away, jamming her foot on the accelerator. Two bullets thudded into the body of the Land Rover. She began to steer a zig zag course to put them off their aim. Another two bullets hit home. Glass smashed; an indicator light she reckoned.

Glancing in the rear view mirror she could see, despite the vibrations, the two hunters stand, rifles hanging by their sides. She was out of range. So were the camels. She could see their dust a couple of miles ahead. They would survive for a little while longer at least, protected by the fastnesses of the Gashun Gobi. In a half hour she would have to stop and take stock of her supplies. With the satellite tracking computer, she would be able to navigate her way out of the desert. But her survival would depend on where the next fuel stop was and whether it was marked on Shackleton's charts. Joy began to wonder just how much she had sacrificed for the camels. She really did not give a damn what happened to Brett or Shackleton or the others. Not even the handsome Mr Bey. She smiled and relaxed back into her seat. It was going to be a long drive.

Sideshow

The Bureau for Psychic Studies was one of the few UN agencies that did not thrive on publicity. There were no fundraising drives; because of the sensitive nature of its work there could not be. It had to survive on a modest grant, contributions to which were solicited, with varying degrees of grovelling and of success, from member governments.

"I hate these meetings."

"That's obvious." Lucas Platt tapped a series of figures into his console. "You're over budget by 214,000 dollars for the last quarter."

Bernhardt Castorman, director of the BPS, stood up and went to the window of his tiny office. "There were a lot of leads to follow up on. Maybe there won't be next quarter. It'll even itself out eventually."

"But it never does, Bernhardt, does it?"

"You're the accountant. I thought it was your job to make the books balance." He turned and leaned against the window ledge.

Platt's fingers continued to play across the keyboard. "I have a responsibility to accurately report the spending of this agency. If you cannot control or justify that expenditure..." He left the sentence hang in a flurry of activity that suggested he had discovered yet another debit to add to the deficit.

"You'd like that, Lucas. You running this place with all the efficiency of one of your accounting programs. Who cares if we locate any talents, what's important is that we work to budget."

Platt sat back from his deck. "It's going to happen. You keep talking about a breakthrough. A major talent. But it's still just talk. Is it any wonder you've been given six months to clean up your act?" He took a stick of gum out of his shirt pocket, unwrapped it and folded it carefully into his mouth. "You're as good as finished, Bernhardt," he said, chewing slowly. "I know you're not capable of changing. You're sloppy. You've no systems. You follow hunches."

"That's what this agency is all about."

"You'd be surprised how many members of the funding committee will be relieved to see someone un-talented in control of the agency."

"Narrow-minded bastards."

Supernormal mental talent had always frightened Joe Public, whether he was prepared to admit it or not, and following the Patterson scandal of '23 he had what he considered a valid reason to be scared and a hook on which to hang his fears. Eugene M. Patterson had been a candidate for the presidency of the United States of America, or would have been following the Republican primaries for which he was considered to be a shoo-in. Until, that is, it was discovered he was a telepath. There was talk that his entire, and substantial, business empire had been built on a foundation of what society considered fraud – insider trading of the worst kind – because he had been inside the minds of opponents and associates. Mind control they screamed with loathing. Unfortunately Patterson thought that an explanation and an appeal on a personal level could still swing the convention back in his favour. He took the podium and attempted to convince his former followers that his telepathy had not been a factor in his political career, though he had to admit to using it to personal advantage in his early days in industry. What Patterson had not considered was the impossibility of persuading people you have not been messing with their minds while they are worrying that it is exactly what you are doing.

Things got out of hand. Badly. Eugene M. Patterson was torn apart by his repulsed former supporters. Joe Public said, *I knew it all along.* Psi talents stayed firmly in the closet. But certain men of vision saw the real future of the race in the power of the mind. Hence the Bureau of Psychic Studies was set up.

Ostensibly its brief was to locate talents and control them for the good of the community; society likes watchdogs. Its real aim was not control but the development of such talent to a level where it could usefully serve the community; if the community could be persuaded to allow it. But the big problem was finding the talents. Like every other member of society they believed that the BPS were interested in locking Psi talents away in institutions and studying them as though they were some sort of vaguely distasteful and sub-human species that had been discovered. Physical investigation of the talented brain for abnormalities was a popular image. It certainly did not help the BPS.

"Bernhardt," Platt said, "you cannot allow your feelings to dictate to you. You can't seriously believe that you will be allowed to go on spending fifty thousand dollars at the drop of a hat to investigate something that feels good to you."

"Why not? That's where all our best scores have come from so far."

"And why your success rate is so poor."

"Bullshit!" Castorman said. "You think your systems can do any better?"

"The committee does."

The intercom on the director's desk buzzed. He slipped back into his chair and answered the call, glad of the opportunity to halt the argument, even temporarily. From the day Platt had been dumped on him, they'd never agreed on anything except maybe a preference for Kenyan Blue Mountain coffee in the office percolator. At first he had thought it was the twenty-five year age gap between him and the accountant. It took him six months to realise that Lucas Platt's ambitious nature would always be a barrier. The accountant was not content with control of the agency's finances, he wanted the directorship for himself.

What hurt Castorman most was that the younger man did not crave the job for its own sake; to Platt it was merely a stepping stone to something better. He was prepared to destroy what Castorman had taken fifteen years to build, without a thought for the consequences to the man or the agency. The director's job was his life; without it he had nothing. He had willingly sacrificed any private life he might have had.

Although he had always been an intensely withdrawn man, had guarded his privacy and his thoughts even more jealously than his un-talented fellows, after setting up the Bureau it was like he had gone out of his way to avoid involvement of any sort, particularly romantic, with the opposite sex in case he might have been diverted from his life mission.

"What!" Castorman snapped into the intercom. His secretary flinched. "Sorry, Elna, what is it?"

"Clifford Breech wants a word with you."

"You know I'm in a meeting."

"He's just gotten off the phone with one of our contacts in England and you said you wanted to hear all reports of activity over there immediately, no matter what."

He glanced at Platt. "Okay, send him in."

"Another hunch?" the accountant said. "You see what I was talking about? If we don't sort out our financial problems for this quarter they might not give you another six months and yet you're prepared to drop everything just cause Madame Zelda from Toad-in-the-Hole saw something in her tea leaves."

The office door opened and Clifford Breech came in. He was a good man, one that Castorman could trust. And he could smell talent.

Breech took a seat and nodded to Platt. As with all the operations staff he was not particularly fond of the accountant, nor was he on anything close to good terms with him. Breech was well aware that if and when Platt took control the first cutbacks would be in Field Ops, and the accountant would not be above taking personal antipathy into account when reducing manning levels.

"Give me the short version," Castorman said. "If it wasn't England we wouldn't even be talking."

Breech smiled. Everyone in the operation was aware of the boss's presentiment that something big was going to break in the British Isles. Of course he had had it almost nine years before. But Castorman still retained faith in it, even if it had become something of a joke amongst the rest of the staff. "Lesley James," he said. "She's a freelance, been on the books for three years, lifter and to a much lesser degree a reader; anyway, she was at a funfair with her boyfriend..."

"Funfair?" Castorman broke in. "I didn't think there were any left."

"What better place to hide freaks?" Platt said.

Castorman turned an ice-cold stare onto the accountant. "We don't consider ourselves freaks."

"Talents don't like to draw attention to themselves," Breech said, attempting to defuse the situation. "And they know we're out there looking, so using their talent at all is dangerous. And if the public discovers that they're not just tricksters, well, they might get away with a beating but then again they might not. There has always tended to be a lot of casual violence at carnivals. Who's going to notice if one of the geeks gets his or her head stoved in?"

"Can we get back to your report, Cliff?" Castorman said.

"Sorry, Bernhardt. Where was I? Lesley at the funfair, yes. So she sees this sideshow, sort of run down, but as they're passing it she gets the tiniest glimmer of psychic energy, either well shielded or vestigial talent. She investigated and reckoned that there was more than one person in the sideshow with talent."

"How many?" the director demanded.

"Eleven," Breech answered uncertainly.

"Eleven?" Castorman whispered.

Platt laughed. "Eleven," he said, as if it was the punchline of the most amusing joke he had heard in years. "She's having you on."

"I'd like to take this one, myself," Breech said.

"No." Platt was suddenly serious. "We've overspent disgracefully so far this year, I won't sanction any more expenditure. Especially not on a wild goose chase to the other side of the Atlantic. I might okay a bus ticket to Des Moines."

"When can you leave, Cliff?" Castorman said.

Platt whirled on the director. "I said no more money and I mean it."

"I'm the director, Lucas, I can override any decision you care to make. Well, Cliff?"

"I swear to you, Bernhardt, if you go ahead with this ludicrous scheme I'm going to the committee and I can guarantee that if I do you're finished. Now. Not in six months time or six weeks time. Now. Today, tomorrow, however soon they can call a meeting."

"When Cliff?" Castorman repeated, ignoring the red faced accountant.

By the middle of the twenty-first century circuses, funfairs and carnivals were an anachronism. There were only two surviving in Britain and both were heavily subsidised by the Arts Council. The one that interested Cliff Breech was doing a two week run at Glastonbury before heading north for a summer season at Whitley Bay. Whatever funding it was receiving, he thought, just wasn't enough. Everything appeared shabby and run down. The shows were lacklustre and the performers dispirited. It made a semi-brave effort at being garish and noisy but it was obvious that hearts were not in it.

Lesley James led him almost apologetically through the maze of seedy tents and stalls. A gypsyish-looking man on the rifle range called to them, unenthusiastically pushing his wares. Anything more than casual scrutiny revealed his gypsy colouring to be theatrical make-up. Breech was sure that even his blackened teeth were artifice.

"This must look really... crummy?" Lesley giggled. "Do they still use crummy?"

"No, but it kind of sums this place up, doesn't it?"

She slipped her arm into his. "We're nearly there," she said, answering his unvoiced question. "We should at least look as if we're out for an evening's fun. I hope you don't object."

"I guess I can put up with it in the line of duty."

Lesley was an attractive woman. She was half a head shorter than him, which he liked; she had dark, nut-brown hair and lots of it, which he very much liked. Her figure was neat and he felt sure that if he placed an arm around her she would fit perfectly. But best of all was her voice which had a soft burr that he could not quite pin down geographically. Being friendly toward her came easily. He wished, even on short acquaintance, that she was not getting engaged in two days. If she had not told him at least he could have entertained some faintly romantic illusions about her.

At the rear of the fair, tacked on like an afterthought, stood two cheerful, candy-striped canvas tents. They were cleaner, in better repair than the remainder of the show, and the incipient air of gloom that had manifested itself the further into the carnival they travelled was dissipated as a musty smell will be by an open window. There was a small crowd gathered outside the flap of the nearer tent. A barker, dressed in a Houdstooth check jacket and cavalry twill trousers topped off by a brown derby, pattered rapidly through his spiel, enthusing his audience with a show of genuine enthusiasm for his wares.

"Weston's Wonderland," Breech read from the banner above the entrance to the tent. "I can almost believe it."

The crowd began to file into the tent in laughing, whispering groups and Breech and Lesley joined the end of the line. Inside, there was virtually total darkness which surprised Breech. Even without interior lighting some vestige of the carnival's gaiety should have shone through the thin canvas.

A single spotlight, mounted over the doorway, blinked on, its bright pool illuminating the smiling barker. He doffed his hat and bowed to the crowd. "Ladeees and gentlemen," he cried, pointing into the blackness at the back of the tent. "The Amaziinnng China George."

The spot snapped off and another, mounted close by and canted at a shallower angle, cut a circle in the void. China George was tall, with straight black hair that shimmered in the light, copper skin and a nose like an eagle's beak. He was dressed in loose pyjamas decorated with dragons and pagodas. But it would have taken a lot more than a costume to make him look Chinese. Breech wondered why he had not simply billed himself as Hiawatha or Geronimo; Amerindians were far more exotic than Chinese, if that was the reasoning behind the stage name.

China George reached into the darkness behind him and produced a long stemmed wine glass. Holding it up into the light, he enfolded it in his enormous hands and squeezed. Although she had seen the act before Lesley could not prevent herself joining the general gasp of surprise as the glass shattered. He opened his fists and showed the audience the jagged shards into which the glass had been reduced, also demonstrating that he was uninjured. Then, with a flourish, he threw back his head and emptied the contents of his hands into his mouth and chewed them with apparent relish.

His next trick involved pushing a sword, which a member of the crowd had tested for sharpness, through his left hand side under the ribs and out through his back. George himself uttered not a single word or sound during the performance. The only voice to be heard was the barker's, uttering calm assurances that there was no danger to the performer nor did he suffer any more than slight discomfort. The secrets of the mystical east were mentioned as were long years of study in a Tibetan monastery.

George completed his act by taking an old fashioned hammer and a nail and driving the latter into the top of his skull with the former.

"Any member of the audience," the barker said in a hushed tone, "who doubts the authenticity of this display may, for a ten pound wager, attempt to pull the nail out of George's head."

Breech was unsurprised when there were no takers. He briefly considered, in the interests of science, taking up the offer himself. But his stomach rebelled at the thought of the resulting gouts of blood should he succeed.

The spotlight strobed briefly and a small, thin man, like a skeleton draped in folds of skin, appeared in George's place. He carried a vessel that resembled a goldfish bowl the size of a large pumpkin, which he placed on the ground. Grinning broadly he bent himself double and placed his head inside the bowl. His shoulders followed, then the rest of his torso, his hips, his legs and, seemingly impossibly, his feet. From where Breech stood he had a clear view of the performer's leering face all the way through the act. As each new body part was forced into the bowl, the man's face was pressed more tightly against the glass sides, flattening and contorting it. There did not seem to be a cubic centimetre of space that was not filled by compacted flesh. Most of the audience were too stunned to clap when China George appeared and carried the vessel and the performer out of view.

"Goddamit!" Breech whispered. "For a second there I thought China George was going to eat him."

Lesley grasped his hand and squeezed. He was glad of that touch of reality.

There were two further acts to follow. The first was an extremely pretty and curvaceous girl in a costume that showed off her assets in an erotic but never vulgar manner, who juggled a selection of unusual objects including four cups of steaming coffee, from which not a drop was spilt, and a selection of live reptiles with excessive amounts of fangs. The second, and the star of the show, was a traditional stage-type magician, The Great Magus, who dazzled the gathering with card and coin tricks, a display of levitation, and delivered a finale which entailed producing fresh flowers from the pockets of his tail coat until he was literally knee deep in blooms.

It was a good note to end on and when he stepped out of the spotlight the crowd applauded warmly and good humouredly. Breech could feel the audience's relief that the highlight had been so mundane in content and execution. Their ability to be amazed had been thoroughly drained. The lights came up and a comedian in a clown suit began a series of rapid-fire jokes, each one worse than the last. Outside, the barker attempted to draw people's attention to the other tent which he claimed held an exhibition of scientific interest for the entertainment and edification of discerning patrons.

"Freak show?" Breech asked Lesley.

She nodded. "It's the only one I've ever seen," she said. "They've never really been popular in England."

Most of the crowd leaving the Wonderland drifted back towards the blare of the main drag. Only a handful of patrons considered themselves discerning.

"Did you feel it?" Lesley asked.

Until that moment Breech had not thought about his mission since entering the sideshow. He had been totally in the thrall of the performers and had forgotten completely about checking for signs of Psi talent. His cheeks flushed.

Lesley, still clinging tightly to his hand, laughed. "I had to go back a second time, myself," she admitted. "But look, you won't be bombarded the same way in the freak show. And you'll have a better atmosphere for checking them out."

"The freaks are talents as well?"

She shrugged. "See what you think."

The second tent was smaller and contained six exhibits, all living. The curiosities, as they were described by the barker – who had turned lecturer for the occasion – were lined around the three walls facing the entrance. Each sat in a straight backed chair, roped off from the public like dinosaur bones in a museum. But none of them was on a par with the performers in the Wonderland. There was a snake-man who had skin textured like a reptile and the markings of a cobra, a fat lady who was indeed grotesquely oversized, a bearded lady with facial hair that would have made Rasputin jealous, Jo-Jo the boy who was born in space with large saucer eyes and a monstrous barrel chest, a genuine hermaphrodite who would display his/her genitals for an extra five pounds, and a wizened creature of indeterminate sex who devoured live mice and frogs.

Breech examined each of the exhibits carefully, his mind wide open attempting to catch any suggestion of psychic energy. In each case there was a vague suggestion of talent but nothing that would normally warrant further investigation. By the time he had satisfied himself that there was nothing startling about the levels, the barker was herding the last viewers outside.

"Move along now," the barker said, guiding him by the elbow towards the exit. "Show's over. Last performance in the Wonderland starting in five minutes. Get your tickets now."

Breech stared thoughtfully after the barker as he moved to the front of the Weston's Wonderland tent to begin drumming up custom.

"What is it?" Lesley asked.

"I'm getting a reading off him as well. Nothing special, but a reading all the same."

"That's why I contacted your office."

"It just doesn't add up. Why would all these minor talents congregate together like this?" Breech looked about. There was a trailer selling burgers and hot dogs almost opposite the sideshow. "I'm starving," he said. "Come on, let's grab a hot dog."

Lesley made a face. "Never got a taste for them. I'd love a bag of chips though. French fries," she added as a momentary look of confusion clouded his eyes.

They purchased their snack and joined the queue for the Wonderland's final performance, eating rapidly as food was discouraged in the tent.

"I've been thinking since I was here last," Lesley said. "About why talents would band together."

"And?"

"Maybe there's some way of joining a load of little talents together to make one big one."

"I suppose it's possible if they all have the same kind of talent, although I've never heard of it being done." The line began to move.

"But it's an angle worth considering."

Watching the show a second time, Breech was able to concentrate on checking out the artistes. Each one of them appeared to be giving off a low level of psychic energy but, as with the freaks, not enough to make them individually interesting. When the performance was over they hung about outside the tent after the barker had collared a handful of punters for his exhibition of scientific interest. The American wanted to talk to one of the performers.

After about ten minutes wait the flap was thrown back and a middle-aged woman appeared brandishing a sweeping brush. She smiled vaguely at the couple and began to sweep out the evening's debris. There was a light on inside the tent and from where they were standing it was obviously empty. Breech wondered how the performers had left; there did not seem to be an exit apart from the one they stood before. He placed an arm around Lesley's waist in a familiar manner and led her over to the woman with the broom.

"Good evening, ma'am," he said in his best Hollywood American-abroad accent.

The woman continued sweeping. "Last show's over," she said without looking up.

"Yes, ma'am. We saw it. It was really something. We were hoping maybe to meet one or two of the artists, just to say hi."

"Sorry, dear," she said. "They'll all be in their trailers."

"Are you," Breech waved a hand at the tents, "part of all this?"

The woman smiled with shy pride. "Well, in a very small way."

"I envy you the freedom of it," Lesley said. "How did you ever get involved with something like this?"

"The Great Magus is my son."

"Magus?" Breech said.

"The star of the show," the woman said, her smile fading.

"The conjurer," Lesley whispered.

"I'm sorry," Breech laughed. "I got so caught up in all of it that by the end I'm afraid I have to admit I was completely ignoring the MC."

The woman's good humour returned, brightening her face. "I'm glad you liked it."

"Liked it? It was... It was wonderful."

"Please, Mrs...?" Lesley began.

"Weston. Molly Weston," the woman supplied.

"Oh, I see. Please, Mrs Weston, couldn't you ask your son just to have a word with us. It would mean so much to Cliff."

"I'm sorry, dear, Albert doesn't talk to anybody." The woman flicked a small pile of dust and chocolate wrappers to the side of the door and stepped back inside closing the flap.

"Wait, Mrs Weston." Breech stepped towards the entrance.

Two things happened at once. Out of the corner of his eye Breech saw a shadow, which he was pretty sure was China George, detach itself from the darkness towards the rear of the tent. Simultaneously a thrill of something akin to naked fear speared through his mind.

Lesley staggered drunkenly and he threw out an arm to steady her.

His own knees had all the strength of whipped cream. They leaned against one another for support.

"The intensity of it," Lesley said.

"That was real power. I've never felt such a strong projection. They must have some way of banding together. We're way out of our league here. I'd better see about getting some back-up."

It was eleven o'clock when they got back to Breech's hotel. He put through a call to New York at once. No matter what the time, the BPS office was always manned. Elna was still on duty at reception. 'Cliff,' she said when his face came on the screen.

The one word spoke volumes. She was relieved to see him, she was worried about him and also about something else. He wished he had time to talk to her. "Put me through to Bernhardt," he said.

"Bernhardt's not here."

Breech cocked an eyebrow at her. Bernhardt practically lived in his office. The Bureau was his life.

"Mr Platt issued instructions that you were to be put straight through to him when you called." Reluctantly she pressed the switch that transferred the call.

He could see that Elna had badly wanted to talk to him but couldn't. Bernhardt would never have authorised a snoop circuit on the phone lines, he said to himself. Would he?

The screen blanked for a moment and Elna's face was replaced by Platt's head and shoulders. He was sitting well back from the phone unit, his feet on the desk and tilting his chair as far back as it would go. For a split second Breech felt disoriented. Platt was in Bernhardt's office, swinging on Bernhardt's chair. It did not take talent to add that one up.

"We're on to something big over here. Something really big," Breech said rapidly. "But I'll need a support team."

Platt shook his head. "All you'll need is a ticket home. Operations have been suspended. All field staff are to report back in A.S.A.P. That includes you. Especially you."

"Aren't you listening? This is it. This is what Bernhardt's been waiting for. A major talent. The big one."

"You're the one who's not paying attention. Read my lips." He spoke evenly. "Field Ops have been suspended. Come in now. That is all." Platt smiled. "You will report to me by five PM tomorrow or you're fired. Is that clear? Not reprimanded. Not suspended. Fired. F.I.R.E.D. Fired. Canned. Given the old heave ho." He was really enjoying this.

Breech cut the connection. Lesley who had watched the whole performance from the side stepped close and placed a hand on his shoulder.

"I'm sorry, Cliff," she said.

He sat in silence, not moving. His thoughts went to Bernhardt who had virtually taken him in off the street and invested his own time and money on developing to its fullest the minor talent of a skinny kid well on the road to delinquency. Bernhardt who had set up the BPS almost single-handed in the face of governmental apathy and public antipathy. Bernhardt who, with a little effort, and if he had been a little less driven, could have found the right woman rather than be staring a lonely old age in the face. Bernhardt, who was worth a hundred Lucas Platts.

"Fuck him," Breech said. "I'm not giving up on this. It's what the Bureau's all about. If we let this one go it means the last fifteen years of Bernhardt's life have been for nothing."

"He said he'd fire you. Didn't he mean it?"

"Platt meant it all right. I just don't give a good goddamn. If he's gotten rid of Bernhardt and is pulling the strings now, then I don't want the job. I wouldn't work for him even if he begged me to stay. Which is highly unlikely, seeing as how he can't abide me."

"So what's your next move?"

"Tomorrow morning I'm going down to the sideshow and I'm going to talk to one of them."

"What time will I meet you?"

"Haven't you got to be at your own job?"

"I can get a day off. They're pretty understanding."

"Okay. Outside the Carney at eleven," Breech said.

*

At eleven-oh-five the next morning they stood on the exact spot that the Wonderland had occupied the night before. Apart from two patches of flattened grass there was no sign that the sideshow had ever been there. The back of the hamburger wagon was open and the owner could be seen polishing his deep fryer. They went over and called through the door.

"The Wonderland," Breech said, jerking a thumb over his shoulder. "How come it's gone?"

"Got a better offer maybe," the man said. "How should I know?"

"But the rest of the carnival...?"

"Wonderland's a concession, just like I am. As long as they pay their fees on time they're welcome to stay. Who knows, perhaps they weren't making money?"

"Any idea where they went?"

"Uh uh!" The man went back to his polishing.

"Could you give us an idea of where they might have gone?" Lesley asked.

"Devon maybe. There's a fair in Taunton this time of year." He pushed his cap back on his head and scratched his crown. "France is good. The Papin brothers are always looking for acts. Italy's not bad. That's about it, love." He thought a moment. "Oh! There's Meagher's show in Dublin. Yeah, I'm pretty sure it's Dublin. If they're not there, then it's Waterford. It's small, but it's got a good reputation. One of the few real independents left."

"Thanks. Thanks a lot," she said.

As they turned away from the burger wagon they noticed a man down on one knee on the Wonderland's former site. Breech recognised him instantly.

"Bernhardt," he called, and walked swiftly to his former boss.

The older man climbed to his feet and brushed loose grass off the knee of his Brooks Brothers suit. He stuck his hand out and Breech shook it warmly.

"This must be Lesley," he said.

She moved alongside Breech and was formally introduced to the former director of the BPS.

"What are you doing here, Bernhardt?" Breech asked.

"Nowhere better to be," Castorman said. "And anyway, this is where the action is."

"How did you find your way here?" Lesley asked.

Castorman tapped the side of his nose. "Used to be called intuition. But we know better." To Breech he said, "Update me."

The former director scuffed the grass at his feet as he listened to what Breech had to say. When the investigator was finished he thrust his hands into his pockets and paced out the Wonderland site.

"Nothing," Castorman said, staring at the ground. "Not even a piece of litter left behind." He glanced at Lesley who was watching him attentively. "I'm like a bloodhound. I need something that belonged to the subject if I'm to track it down."

She rummaged in her handbag and produced a ticket stub. "This enough?"

"Kiss her for me, Cliff," Castorman smiled. "I'm too old for that sort of excitement." He held the ticket stub tightly in his fist and concentrated all his abilities on it. "This is almost hot. There's a lot of power, tightly controlled." He rubbed the stub gently between the tips of his fingers, and squeezed his eyes shut. "Blue," he said.

"What?" Lesley said.

Breech placed a forefinger to his lips.

"Blue," Castorman repeated. "Sky?" He paused. "No sea. Sea, deep and cold. Green." He transferred the ticket to his left hand. "There's white as well. Grass and clouds. Countryside." He hesitated. "No, the green is too pale. The colours are like blocks. And there's another one. It's brighter. Red maybe." He opened his eyes and blinked, like a child awakened in the night. "I dunno. I'm lost. Any of that make any kind of sense to you?"

"You said the colours were in blocks," Breech said. "What shapes?" Castorman gave it some thought. "Rectangles. Sharp and clear. Man made. Straight lines, ninety degree angles at the corners."

"Do you always see things in terms of colour, Mr Castorman?" Lesley asked.

"Bernhardt, please," Castorman said. "And to answer your question, no, not always. And I hardly ever get anything as clear as this. It's like a procession of coloured rectangles."

"A tricolour," Breech said.

"A what?"

"A tricolour. It's a type of flag. Three bars of colour. France's is red white and blue. I'm pretty sure of that."

"No," Castorman said. "The blue is definitely sea. They crossed water, that's what that means. I'm sorry for confusing you. It's not one of the rectangles."

"Italy's is red, white and green," Breech said. "And the guy at the hamburger concession said France, Ireland or Italy."

Castorman was deep in thought. Something was troubling him about the colours. Something was not quite right. Slightly askew. He still wasn't sure that he had all the shades right.

"Ireland's flag is a tricolour as well," Lesley said.

"Really?" Breech smiled. "I wouldn't have known that."

"What colours?" Castorman demanded.

"Green, white and orange."

"Orange. That's it," he said. "Not red, orange." He began to walk away from the empty site. "Well, what are you waiting for, let's go."

"Can I come?" Lesley asked.

"Wouldn't go without you," Castorman said.

"What about your engagement party? Isn't it tonight?" Breech asked.

"I can get engaged any time," she said. "Something like this comes once in a lifetime."

In Dublin it was raining which was nothing unusual. Meagher's carnival was easily tracked to the south city suburb of Booterstown, where it occupied a tiny piece of waste ground between a service station and a row of houses with ground floors converted into shops. The rear of the site looked out picturesquely over a wildfowl preserve onto Dublin bay, but that was about the only positive feature about the location.

That and its availability.

The Weston's Wonderland sideshow was jammed in at the service station side of the site, hard against the rear of an advertising hoarding. It looked somehow smaller and sadder than it had in Glastonbury. The candy stripes seemed a little more faded, the roofs sagged noticeably. There was a hand-painted sign leaning against the front of the Wonderland tent. *First Show, 8.30*, it read.

Bernhardt Castorman checked his wristwatch. It was slightly before eight. "All we've got to do is find one of the show people. It doesn't matter which."

"Maybe we should look for the Great Magus?" Breech suggested. "After all, he appears to own the thing."

"If it's a co-operative effort then any one of them can tell us what we want to know," Castorman said.

They walked openly up to the front entrance of the main tent. Breech pushed aside the canvas flap and went in alone. It was dark inside and he could not find a light switch anywhere, not even the controls for the spotlights. He allowed his eyes time to become accustomed to the gloom.

When they did there was nothing to see. The tent was completely bare. Nothing had been prepared for the first show. As he approached the exit there was a slight commotion outside. He heard a raised voice that he recognised as that of Molly Weston.

"What are you doing snooping about?" she said.

"We merely wish to speak to one of the performers," Castorman said.

Breech pushed his way through the flap.

"I told him and the girl," Molly Weston said. "They don't talk to anybody."

"That's not what you told us," Lesley said.

"Well, it's what I'm telling you now."

"Please, Mrs Weston, if we could just have a few words with your son, I'm sure it would be to his advantage," Castorman said.

The woman laughed, pushing a strand of greying hair out of her eyes.

"You sound like an insurance salesman." Her mood changed in a fraction of a second to one of cool suspicion. "But we know that's not the case, don't we?"

Breech stared at her with interest but kept his mouth shut. He opened his mind to her but failed to register Psi activity, not even the normal background noise most people gave off. The woman hadn't a speck of talent. Her son had not inherited his gift from her. If he was her son. He continued to regard the woman with every shred of concentration he could muster though relying less on his psychic gifts than a more mundane ability to read people through their body language that he had acquired over his years with Bernhard Castorman.

His erstwhile boss possessed the most perfect shielding Clifford

Breech had ever encountered, or heard tell of, and he was as private a person as Breech had ever met. But he had taught himself how to read Castorman's moods and even to some degree his thoughts, through observation.

The woman had no shields but her mind appeared to flit from subject to mundane subject like a mayfly; but nothing her thoughts turned to had any bearing on the current situation. However, her very posture spoke volumes to Breech. One thing was immediately apparent: she had no desire to help them and would lie freely whenever necessary.

"What do we know, Mrs Weston?" Castorman asked.

"Nothing," she said. "I know nothing."

Molly Weston stepped away from them towards the freak show tent. Castorman made to follow her.

"Hold on, Mrs Weston," he said as she disappeared into the tent.

A sudden blast of Psi energy of awesome power stopped him in his tracks. Lesley and Breech experienced it also but not so profoundly. All of them felt weakened, as though their blood sugar level had dropped alarmingly.

"We'll get nothing from her," Castorman said. "But we've got to find the performers. They're obviously linked at this very moment from the level of power we just felt."

They turned away from the Wonderland and began to thread their way back through the guy ropes and tent pegs to the brighter lights of the main attractions. Suddenly Breech stopped.

"Where are we going?" he said.

Castorman looked at him quizzically. "Home, I guess."

"Don't you see, we're being manipulated."

"By this linked group?" the ex-director said.

Breech shook his head. "This is a long shot, but trust me. We're going back to see Mrs Weston."

"Why?" Lesley asked.

"Best you don't know," the investigator said. "If both of you are confused it might just mask me long enough."

"For what?"

"No more questions. Come on."

Breech led them back to the freak show tent. As soon as they got close Molly Weston appeared in the entrance.

"I told you there's nothing here for you," she said.

Breech signalled his colleagues to stop and approached her alone.

"You know who we are, Molly," he said. "We can help. We can train you and put your talent to good use. We can keep you safe. We'll find you a job that pays well. Whatever it is you want, Molly, we can help you do it. The UN has more pull than people think."

"Help me," she sneered, spitting on the ground at his feet.

"You can be among people like yourself for once, Molly. People who can understand you and respect your abilities. You'll be able to show people what you can do, openly."

Breech saw in her face that he was getting to her. "Bernhardt." He waved the ex-director forward. "Open up for reading. Open completely."

"What? What are you talking about? Are you saying this woman has some sort of talent that we can't sense?"

"Trust me, Bernhardt. Open up to her."

"You've got to tell me what's going on," Castorman said.

Breech glanced over at Molly Weston. "You were controlling us, Molly, weren't you? It was you made us just walk away. You reckoned by the time we shook it off you could be long gone."

She pursed her lips noncommittally as if to say, go on, I'm listening; maybe you're right.

"There is no Wonderland, is there Molly? No Magus, no China George, no snake-man." He tapped the side of his skull. "It's all in here, isn't it, Molly. You created it with the power of your mind and made it all work. I'm right, aren't I?"

She stared evenly at him, the beginnings of a smile melting the coldness in her eyes and softening the line of her mouth.

"The performers were psychic projections which is why we got a low level talent reading off them all. But they were so good that they even had us fooled. And your shielding was perfect, which is why we couldn't sense you. I've never come across anything like it."

He glanced over to his ex-boss. "That's what tipped me as to what was going on. Her shields were too good."

"When I thought about what I felt when I tried to probe you," he said to Molly, "there was nothing. A void. And finding someone with absolutely no Psi energy is even more unusual that finding a strong talent. Everybody's got some level of talent, even if it's useless to all intents and purposes. Either I'm as wrong as anybody's ever been or you're the best there is."

Lesley could see the woman slowly warming to Cliff Breech. Even Psi talents were prone to flattery.

Breech turned to Castorman. "Let her read you, Bernhard. Show her what the Bureau means to you. What it could mean to her. Show some trust. Reach out to her."

Bernhardt Castorman was having difficulty in keeping his jaw from dropping. Gaping was particularly unattractive in older men. If Breech was right this woman was the most powerful talent that had ever been found. Not only that, she was more powerful than anybody had even imagined possible.

He felt a gentle probing at the edge of his consciousness. If Breech was right this woman was the most important thing that had ever happened to him. If Breech was right she could save his career and put the Bureau on a far stronger footing with the committee. He looked at her more closely. She wasn't as old as he had initially thought. In fact she was a good five years younger than himself, if he was any judge. And not at all bad looking. No sir. Pretty damn good, if the truth be told. Bernhardt Castorman grinned broadly and opened up his inmost secrets to the enormity of Molly Weston's talent.

The Great Eddie Clarke Farewell Tour

The backup band pumped out the spiky rhythms of what Eddie Clarke liked to call White Man's Soul. The dancing bodies at the foot of the stage looked as though they had been filmed on an old-time newsreel camera: jerky, uncoordinated, at the wrong speed. Out beyond the lights, another twelve thousand rabid fans jostled one another in attempted motion.

'Can't stand still'. It was what he always said at the start of a concert. It was the title of his third album. Twelve thousand pairs of feet tended to agree with his sentiment.

Eddie Clarke was a phenomenon. Four albums under his belt in under three years, all platinum. Every date on every concert tour sold out since his first hit. The music press had attempted to dismiss him as 'merely a singer'. That quote had headlined a piece in the *New York Times*. If the facts that he didn't play an instrument or write songs were important, then it was true: Eddie was just a singer. But what a singer. What a voice. And what a performer.

His fans loved him. He lived for them, and for success. He was born poor and dragged himself up through the dog eat dog world of showbusiness as much by the power of his will to succeed as by the enormity of his talent. He was a man driven to get to the top. Some day he would be as big as Elvis. Bigger. Now that was something worth aiming for.

If his band, his manager, and the rest of his retinue were less than fond of him as a person it was down to the single-mindedness with which he approached his assault on the music business. He didn't have time to be a nice guy. A single lifetime was hardly enough to achieve what he wanted. Everything had to be sacrificed to fuelling the realisation of his ambition.

Eddie stepped forward into the spotlight that always focused on his mike. He feinted at the mike stand, then stepped forward, bent at the waist and shook the soaking coils of his lank black hair over the front rows. A thousand teenage girls screamed. Several of them regretted not going to the bathroom before the show. Eddie Clarke grinned and picked up a sodden towel, wiping it across his face.

He couldn't remember it ever being so hot on stage before. He reckoned he had lost at least half a stone in moisture alone. Every part of him was wet. One more number and he was going to have to get off stage and at least change his jeans.

The lead guitarist hit a power chord, bass and drums hesitated for two beats, Eddie stepped square into the spotlight again, the band crashed into overdrive. Eddie screamed into the mike and grabbed the stand. The world slewed sideways into slow motion. He could feel the first touch of metal against the palm of his hand, the first burn of the electricity as it punched along his arm towards his chest. A giant hand squeezed his heart. His feet left the floor and he arched backwards, the killer mike stand still gripped tightly in his blackened fingers. Another legend of rock 'n' roll was about to pay the ultimate price for his fame.

Eddie Clarke sat up in complete silence. The stage was scattered with instruments, speakers and cables, but devoid of musicians. A single set of hands clapped somewhere past the array of lights at the front of the stage. Eddie shaded his eyes with his unburnt left hand but could see no-one. A lone figure coalesced through the blinding whiteout. At first just a silhouette, the figure solidified into a man in his middle thirties, slicked back hair, sharp blue suit, sunbed tan. Eddie's first thought was: agent. Wait for the smile, he said to himself.

The man walked slowly to the edge of the stage, still clapping. He smiled about fifty thousand dollars worth of bridgework. Eddie nodded. Agent, sure enough. The man stopped clapping and vaulted onto the stage. Eddie wished he would stop smiling; the lights were bad enough without his help.

"Welcome, Eddie," the agent said, sticking out his hand. Eddie was unsure whether it was to help him to his feet or part of the greeting.

"Welcome where?" Eddie said, ignoring the hand. He stood up and began to brush at the seat of his jeans.

"You've been called, Eddie."

"Called?" Eddie's head felt as though it was stuffed with wet tissue paper. He was sure he could feel some of it hanging out of his ear. It was difficult to think straight. Where had everybody gone? How could they have gone? He must have been unconscious for hours. But then, why would they leave him on stage. Shit, there were enough of them relying on him for their meal ticket. He shook his head, attempting to clear the head-cold feeling behind his sinuses, trying to get the old grey matter working smoothly again. "Called by who?" he asked, a whine creeping into his voice.

"By whom," the agent smiled.

Eddie was beginning to worry that something was badly wrong. No matter how slow his thought processes, he could not think of a single eventuality that would adequately explain his current circumstances. And the agent's smirk was giving him a right pain in the neck. He knew it was the price of fame, but 'hair oil' here was just one obsequious git too many.

It was definitely time to go home, shake himself clear of the bloodsuckers. Maybe organise that homecoming tour he'd been talking to Chas about, around the pubs and clubs in the north of England, back to his roots. Could be just the right career move. Demonstrate what a man of the people he was. How much more important the fans were than money. Do a documentary on it. Brilliant publicity. Why couldn't Chas think of stuff like this? What did he pay him for?

"There's no easy way to put it, Eddie," the agent said. "So I'll give it to you straight from the hip." He paused for a count of four. "You've passed over to the other side, Eddie."

"You mean I'm dead?"

"Most of us are, over here." The agent laughed at his own joke.

For some reason the idea didn't come as a shock. Nor did he feel any immediate urge to refute the claim. He looked slowly about the deserted stage. It appeared to be the place he had been performing a handful of minutes before but Eddie had to admit to a certain sense of dislocation. He carefully examined his right hand. A lot of the flesh had burned off his palm. Eddie was sure the white he could see through the mess was bone. So why, if he was still alive, was there no pain.

Dead. That one word said a hell of a lot. More than all the lyrics in all the songs on all his albums. On all of anyone's albums. It was kind of a definitive word. And Eddie was quite certain it defined his present state. It was certainly the only satisfactory way of explaining everything. For the moment. Maybe in time he would think of something else.

"Has it sunk in?" the agent asked.

Eddie nodded hesitantly. It hadn't, but he did not feel overmuch like discussing it. Death was not something he had ever much considered. He was thirty-one years old. He had an entire lifetime before him. Until ten minutes ago.

"Good. Doesn't always. Not immediately. Even though the certainty's been planted."

Eddie nodded again. "Planted," he repeated. Yes, that was it. Someone or something – although he was not a Catholic he was tempted to cross himself and might have if he'd known how – someone had planted the acceptance of death in his mind.

"You've got the advantage of me," Eddie said, holding out his hand.

The agent shook hands. "Sam," he said. "Sam Goldfish."

"You ever think of changing that?" Eddie asked.

"Once," Goldfish said. "In another life."

"So what now?"

Goldfish jerked a thumb towards the wings. "We'd better go and get you checked in."

They exited stage left, down a short flight of steps and along a poorly illuminated corridor. The stage door opened onto a broad street bathed in bright sunshine. There were theatres on both sides of the busy thoroughfare interspersed with cafes, restaurants and bars. Eddie guessed from the angle of the sun it was mid-afternoon, but even at this early hour every venue seemed to be open for business and packed out.

People bustled by on both sides of the street, some seeming to hurry to important appointments, others strolling at ease as though deciding which of the shows they wanted to see or where they wanted to eat.

The theatre directly across the street had a huge poster up which said, *This Week Only, Two Shows A Nite plus Matinee – The One And Only Sam Cooke*. Further along a sign proclaimed that River Phoenix and Orson Welles were starring in a new play by Joe Orton. Eddie stepped into the street to get a better angle on the sign, catch the name of the play. Sam grabbed his elbow and hauled him bodily back onto the pavement as a trolley car rattled past within inches of his nose.

"Just 'cause you're dead doesn't mean you can stop being careful," Goldfish said.

"I'm already dead. What's the worst can happen to me?"

"You mess up here, by say, getting yourself run down in the street, there's other places, worse places they can send you."

"They?" Eddie said.

Goldfish pointed towards the sky. Eddie looked up. The clouds had formed some odd shapes. He could see the faces of a couple of bearded old men and one quite stunning woman old enough to be mature but young enough to be interesting. If she were real, Eddie would definitely have got his manager to arrange an introduction after the show. But of course, there was no show any more; he had no manager. What a shame. He stared wistfully at the cloud face. She seemed to be smiling.

"Careful, Eddie," Goldfish said. "You don't want to annoy them."

"What?" Eddie looked from the sky back to Goldfish. "What are you babbling about, Sam?"

"Look at their faces, Eddie. Whatever's going through your mind, they don't like it."

"Who for..." he was going to say Chrissakes but thought better of it, given his current situation, "... for the love of Mike?"

"Them." Goldfish was again pointing upwards.

The old-man cloud-faces had darkened and did indeed look angry. The woman winked at him.

"You don't need enemies this soon," Goldfish said. "We don't even know who called you yet." He took hold of Eddie's sleeve and led him along the street. "Stop looking up."

"What's going on, Sam?"

"Don't look up. They're part of the group that runs this place."

"I thought God..."

"Yeah, well you thought wrong. Sure, he's part of it, but so are the old gods and the others."

"Old gods? Others?"

"It's got something to do with belief systems. Every god that ever had followers gets a say in what happens up here. Number of believers equates to weight of say."

"Then the Christian god, the one God, must carry a lot of weight. He's been around thousands of years."

"You'd be surprised how few real believers there are," Goldfish said. "Come on, we don't have all day. We've got to get you down to artists' registration and check out your sponsor."

"My sponsor?" Eddie was beginning to feel like a machine designed to ask stupid questions.

Goldfish's face tightened into a blank mask. No emotion showed. "The one who called you."

Eddie stopped walking. Goldfish took a further two paces and jerked to a halt. "Hold it a minute," Eddie said. "Are you telling me that I didn't just die because my number was up? I'm dead because somebody up here or," he pointed upwards, "up there, wants me dead?"

"Don't even consider resentment, Eddie. Your sponsor is about the only one in authority who has your welfare at heart."

"So much so that they had me killed?"

"Eddie, get your thoughts straight. It's important. Please." Goldfish tugged at his arm again.

"I'm going nowhere until I get some answers."

Goldfish looked around. Suddenly he appeared shifty, like the classic agent type from fiction and drama, the kind of guy you wouldn't buy a used car from. "Please, Eddie." He stared back the way they had come for a long moment then turned to Eddie. "You'll get me into trouble."

"Tell me what's going on, Sam."

"Okay." He looked cowed.

"Everything?"

"Yes. We'll talk while we walk." Eddie relented and allowed himself to be led. "It's not far. Let's cross the street."

They stopped on the edge of the pavement. Like a good little boy, Eddie looked right, then left, then right again. The traffic was on the wrong side of the road so he looked left again as well. Eddie couldn't help noticing the buildings that stretched both ways into the distance. It was like New York's Broadway and London's West End and every other theatre district in the world all strung out along the one highway. And the traffic was a mixture of everything that has ever served to carry man in peacetime, from cars to wagons pulled by oxen. A 'D Type' Jaguar in British racing green livery pulled an outrageous overtaking manoeuvre on a trolley car. The traffic seemed to still for a congratulatory moment. Eddie thought he heard someone calling his name. It was a female voice. Goldfish placed a hand in the small of Eddie's back and eased him through the temporary lull to the other side of the street.

There were less pedestrians on this side as it was deep in shadow so Goldfish was able to set an increased pace. He seemed less uneasy at a near trot. "Look, Eddie, you've got to take a philosophical view of things. You've been called to a better place. They've lifted you out of the rat race of life on Earth, that vale of tears."

"I liked the rat race, Sam. I was winning."

"How old are you? Twenty-five, twenty-six? You think they're going to call you this early, you're a loser?"

"Would you believe I'm thirty-one," Eddie said, a broad grin creasing his face. "My publicist used to claim twenty-four."

"You just get your thinking right. They can read minds."

Eddie thought he heard the voice again and looked back over his shoulder. As Goldfish led him off the street he could have sworn he heard the sound of running behind. They went quickly along a corridor and down two flights of stairs into a smoky cellar. There was condensation on the bare brick walls and the heat was intense. The bar was along the far wall and at the left end was a small stage. A four piece jazz combo etched sombre melodies while an overweight black woman crooned a blues number. As his eyes became accustomed to the gloom Eddie scanned the faces at the scatter of tables between him and the bar. "Is that...?"

Goldfish pushed Eddie into a seat at a vacant table. "Sit there and don't move. I'll get you registered."

Eddie stared at his guide's back as Goldfish weaved his way through the tables to the bar. He leant across the counter and said something into the barman's ear. The barman nodded his head towards the small stage.

"Bessie just keeps on getting better."

Eddie twisted in his seat towards the voice which was behind him. Its owner was in his late seventies, skeletally thin and sporting a bushy white beard. His eyes were flat and glassy, like a stuffed animal's.

"Mind if I sit?"

"Be my guest." Eddie stared intently at the newcomer, sure he recognised him from somewhere. "Hackney Empire, 1991?" Eddie said.

"Wrong decade." The American country twang in his voice made Eddie reconsider.

A waitress slouched over. Her sunken eyes looked as though they needed white powder to put life into them. "You wanna drink?" she said.

"Could you get me a white wine spritzer, please," Eddie said.

The waitress threw back her head and laughed, slapping her side for effect. "You hear that?" she said, addressing the room. "Spritzer?" A couple of muffled laughs accompanied her display. "Hey, man," she said, "you wanna drink or what?"

Eddie struggled to meet her gaze. "You got coffee?"

"What kinda joint you think this is? A course we got coffee."

"Black, one sugar," Eddie said.

"I'll have Tequila and a bottle of Heineken," the bearded man said.

"Get lost," the waitress said, turning back towards the bar. "Your credit's no good."

"Worth a try," the bearded man said, grimacing.

"I'll get you one," Eddie said.

"Don't work like that."

Someone at a nearby table shouted at them. "Leave the kid alone, Hank." Eddie squinted through the smoke at the bald, black dude that had spoken. He seemed familiar.

A petite young woman in a black mini skirt and a short sleeved blue mohair sweater elbowed her way in front of Hank. She pushed a strand of black hair away from her eyes, pulled up a chair and sat.

"Don't mind me," Hank said.

She ignored the old man, speaking rapidly as she did so. "You've got to come with me, Eddie. Every minute you stay here gives you less chance of getting out."

"You from the rival team, or something?"

"No, I'm from this side all right, but you shouldn't be here. Not yet."

"What the hell are you babbling about? Who are you anyway?"

"How did you get here?" she asked him.

"You answer my questions first."

"Eddie, you're dying. This is not a dream, whatever you might think."

"I never thought it was a dream. I know exactly what's going on." He held up his burnt hand. "I was electrocuted on stage." He turned the hand over and looked at his watch. "Less than an hour ago. I'm dead."

"You're not dead."

"Look, I don't know who you are or why…"

The mini-skirted woman threw herself sideways onto the floor as a chair flew through the space she had just been occupying. Eddie glanced towards its point of origin. Sam was running towards him. He slowed to grab another empty chair. The woman scrambled to her feet and stepped behind Eddie. "Leave him, Goldfish. He's not for you."

"Butt out. I got him first."

"Eddie," she whispered, "you're still alive. There's a team of doctors onstage with your body, trying to revive you. You've got to get back there before they give up."

Without taking his eyes off Goldfish he said, "So what's his angle?"

"He's an agent. He must have a client interested in your talents."

"If you're so keen to save me why weren't you there instead of him when….?"

"I'm sorry. I should have been. I… I got delayed. Listen, come with me. What have you got to lose. If I'm lying you can just come back to Sam."

Goldfish was no more than two feet from Eddie's face. "Don't listen to her. I can get you fixed up but there's a time frame to be observed. If you don't come now, I might not be able to help later. You don't want to end up like Hank, do you?"

Eddie's attention turned involuntarily to Hank for a moment. The old man looked crumpled and empty. If there was a fate worse than death then surely Hank was suffering it.

Eddie felt the woman's hand closing on his arm. She began to pull at him. He was surprised how strong she was. His feet shuffled backwards to maintain his balance. Sam snarled and walked after him. "You don't want to go with her," he said. "This is going to be your big break."

"I'm offering you life," the woman said. "How much bigger a break can you get?"

"You're going to be the man. Everybody'll be looking up to you."

"But you'll be dead. And you don't have to be."

Eddie stopped, pulling his arm free. "Hold it."

"You've no time, Eddie," the woman said.

"Sam, you told me I was dead. Right?"

"What?" A horrified expression passed across the woman's face. "You lied?" Sam Goldfish's features took on the blank mask look again. "He can't lie. None of us can." She turned to Eddie. "He told you that you were dead?"

Eddie nodded.

"He said the words, 'you're dead'?"

Eddie thought about it for a moment. "I thought he did."

To Goldfish she said, "Tell him that your name is... Joe Smith. Tell him that and I'll leave him to you."

"See, Eddie," Goldfish said, "she's getting desperate."

"We can't lie, Eddie. I can't lie." She glared at Goldfish. "Deny it if you're able."

Goldfish remained implacably silent.

"See. I'm telling the truth, Eddie. You're still alive. Dying, but still alive. Now come with me."

Eddie glanced from Goldfish to the woman and back again. He wanted her to be telling the truth. Why should he trust an agent, all they ever wanted was a percentage of you. Just because he was in the hereafter didn't necessarily mean that had changed. He looked the woman in the eye. "Okay, let's go."

She smiled with relief and took him by the hand. They ran back to the street. Everything except for them was moving sluggishly. The traffic seemed suspended in syrup. There were no pedestrians in evidence. "Run," she said, breathing hard.

They ran at her best pace all the way back to the theatre. She pushed him along the centre aisle and onto the stage. His breath came in gasps. His side pained him. He felt disoriented. Standing was difficult. He slumped to his knees. Then, going onto all fours, he turned back to the woman. She was gone. The auditorium was dark. And it was cold. So very cold. His hands had become numb. And his knees. He could no longer be sure if he was still on all fours. Perhaps he had fallen onto his face. He could no longer see and all sensation had drained from his body. He could not even tell which way was up.

The tiny figure in the black mini-skirt rocked back onto her heels. All around her people stood and stared at the stricken figure of Eddie Clarke. It was as though she was the only one who cared. She bent over him again, alternately massaging his heart and administering mouth to mouth. For a third or fourth time she paused and screamed for another doctor to help her. Surely she couldn't be the only person in the theatre with a medical qualification.

"Where's the medical officer?" she demanded.

A road manager shrugged helplessly. "I called an ambulance. They'll be here in minutes."

"He doesn't have minutes." She needed a hypo full of adrenaline. Both of them would benefit from a shot. Her medical bag was in her car. Maybe there was something in it that would make a difference. It might be worth the risk. He was dying by inches. Without some sort of intervention she was going to lose him anyway. It was hopeless. She felt tears running down her face. It was sheer frustration. He didn't have to die. "Damn!" She wasn't going to give up on him.

She reached towards a mic stand to balance herself while she stood. A hand intercepted hers, grabbing her by the wrist. The road manager hauled her upright. "We don't need two casualties," he said.

"What?" She felt she should know what he was talking about but he might as well have been speaking a foreign language.

"The stand is still live."

"Oh." She felt stupid. The jolt of electricity from the defective stand was what had stopped Eddie Clarke's heart in the first place. How could she have forgotten its dangers. And why had nobody killed the power before someone else got hurt. "Get someone to switch the power off," she said to the roadie.

He waved at a figure off in the wings. "That's under control as of..."

"No," she said. "Stop him." There was an aura of control about her. He obeyed without question, like one of Pavlov's dogs salivating on demand. "Here's what I want you to do."

The roadie listened intently as she rapidly outlined her plan. "Got it," he said, and sprinted off stage.

When the roadie was in place the woman in the mini-skirt picked up a guitar and threw it at the live mic stand. The stand toppled and fell across the prone figure of Eddie Clarke. As it slammed into his chest she made a chopping motion with her hand and the roadie threw the switch that cut the power running to it. Eddie Clarke arched his body, like a fish cast onto the deck of a boat. She pushed the stand clear and placed her head against his chest. Faintly, she could hear a heartbeat. His chest heaved and he took a deep, laboured breath. Suddenly the stage was alive with technicians and band members. Everyone wanted to help. The woman in the mini-skirt found herself engulfed. Suddenly, she very badly needed fresh air.

Within minutes of his second electric shock Eddie was sitting up drinking a glass of water. Everyone wanted to talk to him. Everyone wanted to know if he was all right. Someone asked him what it was like to be so near to death.

"I had some pretty weird dreams," he said.

"Better than acid?"

There was a lot of laughter. Everyone was relieved that a potential tragedy had been averted. They wanted Eddie's reassurance that everything was okay. That normal life could resume.

"I dreamed I was called to the other side and some guy wanted me to die, an agent, so that he could carve his ten percent out of my skin."

"Hey, that was no dream. That's real life."

Everyone laughed again.

"Then this chick in a black mini-skirt came along and saved me." He laughed but nobody joined in.

Everybody looked about but the doctor was gone. "The chick in the mini-skirt was here, Eddie. She was the doctor. She saved you."

"Blue sweater?"

"Like something from the sixties, yeah."

Although Eddie demanded his people find her, this was one wish that would remain unfulfilled. It was as though nobody had really seen her. Only Eddie could give any sort of description of her, and he had been unconscious at the time. After a while he convinced himself that he had not been fully out. He must have come around for a moment and seen her. That was the obvious answer. The only answer. The answer that satisfied Eddie.

But he always felt that he would meet his angel in the mini-skirt again. Somewhere.

Hungry Eyes

The mutant needed me. I had been in the game while it was still legal; good enough to avoid brain damage, lucky enough to get out while I was still in control. Lucky, if that's what you call getting your leg crushed in a hit-and-run. There wasn't much wrong that would have given trouble to a competent surgeon but my profession put me beyond the medical insurance pale. The cutter I could afford was more at home with late abortions and sub-legal implants than reconstructive surgery. But he saved the leg, mostly, for which I suppose I should be grateful.

When the mutant found me I had just about touched rock bottom. For months I had been selling blood, turning tricks for freaks on a scar-tissue or mutilation kick, and hiring myself out as a subject for pharmacological experiments. The last of my cash was gone, my body had acquired a toxic build-up that neither the blood nor drug people could ignore any longer and although the smell of terminal decay attracts a particular type of punter I had no stomach for that.

I saw him at the bar drinking on credit and hit on him. He bought, we drank, I talked. As long as he went on buying I went on talking. Eventually, as the weight of alcohol and empty words affected me, I got around to the only subject I really knew: fighting. For the first time the mutant looked at me closely. I could feel him peering beyond the grime, the crippled leg and the emaciation. He was still staring at me when I passed out.

I woke up to bright painful sunlight and the stab of a spring from the body of the couch I had been dumped on. The mutant had two rooms in a rambling, Georgian ruin near the centre of town: Darlington I think; somewhere in the north-east anyway. The room where I woke was crammed with furniture, mainly broken or incomplete. The only clear space was around a two-ring gas burner, perched to one side of an aluminium sink unit, above which a line of food shelves stretched to the crumbling cornices, twelve feet up.

Someone had gone to the trouble of removing my shirt and jeans before lying me out. I lifted my bad leg off the couch and hurried it into my greasy denims, the hydraulics hissing as I shoved the mostly-flesh foot into its boot. I pulled on my damp shirt reluctantly and pushed my way through the jumble of wood and fabric to the kitchen area.

I didn't see the girl arrive. She nodded toward the tea pot and I searched out another cup. The first thing that struck me about her was the way she shone as though she had just stepped out of a shower. In the squalor surrounding us she had no right to look untarnished.

"My name is Armelle," she said in an accent that was carefully neutral but bore an unmistakable trace that placed her origins in Eastern Europe. She didn't look Slav, so she was probably a Russian refugee, or more likely her parents were. She smiled uncertainly.

"Sorry," I said, handing her a cup of tea. "Matt. Matt Lawless."

"One for Brick also," she said.

I raised an eyebrow.

"Our benefactor." A gesture took in the whole flat.

I poured a third cup and followed her through the junk to a door lurking behind a mound of discarded chairs at the far side of the room. It gave onto another, huge and empty except for a bed that looked as if it would sleep ten and a wardrobe capable of housing a family. The mutant was draped across the bed; ugly, naked and hairless bar a mat of bristle on the top of his skull. He reached out a hand for the tea.

"I can fight," he said, over the outstretched hand.

I gave him his cup and sat on the edge of the bed. He waited for me to respond as I sipped my tea and looked him over. He was six feet tall but looked less because of his bulk; muscular and slab-sided, as though he'd been erected by a bunch of navvies without reference to the plans. Nobody had told them he was supposed to be ten inches taller. Maybe they were short of scaffolding.

"You know fighting," he said, presenting a massive fist for my inspection. "You can teach me."

He rolled from his side onto his stomach. Wordlessly the girl climbed onto the bed and straddled his back. She looked like a child compared to him. Her tea cup was gone and in its place was a jar of mustard-yellow cream which she began to knead into his shoulders. I took a final gulp of tea and stood up.

"I don't think so."

My head knew where I wanted to go but seemed reluctant to pass the message to my legs.

Brick grinned decayed teeth up at me. "You know what I am?"

Not until that moment. He looked fringe-normal; enough that he could pass anything but a detailed inspection. I tried to leave again, just to make sure, but with no more success. He was a mutant and he wanted me. The bonding must have taken place while I was unconscious. The girl should have been enough to clue me in. What reason could a looker like her have for hanging round a piece of shit like him in a pit like this?

The mutant's mottled grin stayed in place. His face looked like that of a small boy loose in a toyshop. "When do we start?"

I was feeling washed-out from the night before but spiteful enough to live with background nausea. "Get dressed," I said. "I'll be back in an hour." I stopped in the doorway. "And I'll need some money."

"Where are you going?"

"Fighters need stuff. And special food," I added, with a stroke of inspiration which convinced me there was something still working upstairs. "A diet."

He nodded at the girl. She climbed off him and reached under the bed, producing a crumpled brown paper bag. From it she took a thin bundle of ten credit notes. "How much?"

"Fifty, at least."

She counted off five notes and replaced the rest, which looked about the same again. I hoped he had a way of getting more because it was going to take months to make him a fighter, if it was possible. It takes more than fists like hams and a thick skull.

"You're going to need some sort of punchbag," I said, opening the door. "Maybe some of the spare cushions from in there. Tied together or something. I don't know. You work it out." I paused. "And you'll need to clear this room."

"I can make space," the mutant said.

"If you can stand the smell. But I wouldn't want to sleep where I train." I slammed the door behind me.

I bought the mutant a couple of steaks, as much fruit as I could carry, bandaging for his fists and some training aids: skipping rope, medicine ball, that sort of thing. The rest of the fifty I spent on drinking myself into a fit state of insensitivity to become a trainer. I didn't like the mutant but neither did I dislike myself enough to be able to enjoy the pain he was letting himself in for. I could turn him into a fighter – I could maybe turn him into a winner – but with his build, no matter how well he moved comparatively, he was going to have to walk through an awful lot of punches. If I had thought arguing would do any good or if I had not been already past caring, for myself or anybody else, I might have deflected him. But I felt as if I was inhabiting my own past, living events that had already taken place.

The mutant was a carpenter and could turn his inelegant hands to the intricacies of upholstering. During the days we trained and at night he fixed furniture which the girl sold off a stall in a street market. We did okay.

I lived for the nights. The mutant worked contentedly on his furniture, humming nursery rhymes under his breath. The girl and I sat and talked, splitting a bottle when there was money for it, content just to be in one another's company when we were broke. I came to respect Brick. He was single-mindedly dedicated to the job at hand, whatever it was: training, restoring chairs, eating, loving Armelle. Occasionally I would sit with Brick; mostly when I needed to talk. Once in a while I would ask him questions – about his past, his family, his dreams – which he would do his best to answer. Even the big one.

"Why do you want to give all this up," I asked, late one night after Armelle had gone to bed.

Brick laid down the chair-leg he was working on and looked into my eyes, his brows knitting together. "I don't want to, Matt," he said, shaking his head.

"You know you're going to have to when the fights come."

"Yes."

"Seems to me, you've got everything a man could need right here."

"Mutant," he said quietly.

"I stand corrected. But man or mutant, you're comfortable here. And happy, and safe."

"No, Matt. I mean..." He paused for a while sorting out his thoughts. "What I meant was that I am a mutant. That is the reason I cannot be content."

I began to speak but he held up one of his huge hands.

"Please. Let me finish," he said. "I have at best another five years left to me. I am already nearing thirty years old. Few of my kind live much longer."

"You're fit. And strong."

"That's why I feel I could have as much as five more years."

I nodded. Who was I trying to kid? If he was as old as he said five years was optimistic.

"I must leave Armelle something for afterwards. Some money. Money will protect her. That's why I must fight." He let out a long sigh. "And why I will win."

It was unusual for a mutant to feel deeply for one he has bonded to him. At that moment I pitied him more than I did myself. But not for too long. At least he had the girl.

I did have Armelle to myself for long stretches but there was no way I could be more than a friend; their bonding was too tight. In that one respect I envied him. It may be unnatural by most people's standards but he had the girl in a way I doubted I could ever have any woman. Lying on my couch in the darkness I often fantasized that one day the bond would be broken. I dreamed of leaving, of taking her with me. In my dreams I was tall and straight, my leg was whole. But somehow I knew that it would make no difference to her, only to me.

The mutant was a willing subject for my teaching, limited in what he could achieve only by his less than modest intellect. He grasped the basics well and worked at them endlessly, but the finer points of the art of fist fighting were as far beyond him as speech is to a goat. He had staying power, a punch in either hand that could poleaxe an elephant and a chin like the Sphinx. All he lacked was control. In the early days of training he had come close to damaging his fists because he felt he had to put everything into every punch, to go at top speed from the start and maintain it until he dropped. Bonding works both ways. I could supply the control he needed though it was difficult and tiring. It was like hanging onto a team of horses that have been spooked: it's possible, but they will eventually pull your arms out of their sockets.

When the mutant was finally ready it was up to me to arrange fights. It meant putting my ear to the ground, finding out where the right people were and showing them my face for a while, becoming part of the scenery. Looking the part was important so I got a new suit of clothes, and Armelle to hang on my arm.

We went to the right clubs, taking that month's drug, drinking the right brand of Tequila. The continuous interchange of darkness and glaring light took some getting used to. The monochromatic haze of Brick's sepia-tint rooms and the grainy, bleak greyness of the narrow streets were difficult to shake off. The noise was alien. Spikey machine music with an android disco beat in nine-eight time. The laughter and forced smiles of hopeless faces wanting to be noticed. Goods for sale at every table, leaning against every wall. I recognised the punters, or at least the types. The hungry eyes, the manicured nails, the custom made shoes. Watching them made me feel unclean. How quickly I had forgotten.

Making contact took only a couple of weeks. The promoters, always looking for new blood, were easy to find. Out of place and complacent. Ten years too old, a thousand years too conservative. Cigars and Scotch instead of tequila and wire. A different kind of hunger.

The fight took place in a warehouse. The loading bay had been cleared and some of the racking dismantled to make room for spectators. High in the roof a series of spotlights were fixed to cross girders bathing the entire arena in stark impersonal brightness. At five hundred credits a time the promoter was expecting no more than a hundred takers. It was not a particularly attractive fight; Brick was an unknown quantity expected merely to decorate the concrete with his blood. The purse was ten percent, of which our opponent, a mongrel called Kerslake, got half as appearance money. Our contract was for expenses only – a grand to cover doctor's fees – unless we won. The rules were simple. The last man on his feet was the winner. No kicking. No action on the ground. No rounds. One minute for recovery after a knockdown.

The other fighter was smaller and lighter than Brick but moved well and had a reputation for dirt. For ten minutes the mutant tracked him around the circle made by the spectators, grinding forward continuously, taking punishment, landing the occasional blow. Kerslake retreated steadily, up on the balls of his feet, jabbing his left venomously into Brick's face.

Keeping the mutant's head down and his hands up was a real effort. Preventing him swinging wildly took the rest of my concentration. Bubbling beneath his phlegmatic plodding I sensed an anger at the world for what it had done to him. For denying him a place, for keeping him on the outside, for making him ugly. For making him a mutant. An anger fuelled by each stinging jab, each catcall from the restless crowd.

Despite his months of training and natural fitness, the mutant tired fast. Kerslake was difficult to find; for every shot Brick landed another ten sailed harmlessly past his ducking, shifting frame. With fifteen minutes gone the mutant was fighting my control as much as his opponent. He wanted to be free of the orthodoxy of stance I imposed upon him; the tight defence, measured step and patient probing that limited the damage Kerslake could affect. He began to ape the other fighter's bobbing, swaying head movement as much from fatigue as intent. It was an unexpected benefit and I had more important things to worry about.

Three times in succession Kerslake whipped over rapid-fire combinations. The last punch was a left cross that would probably have crushed the mutant's nose. He ducked into it, taking the impact high on his forehead. The sound of Kerslake's hand breaking was audible throughout the warehouse. A howl of consternation swelled from the spectators. Without a pause for breath it transformed into the baying of a pack. Any blood would suffice. In the end it didn't matter who won.

I held the mutant on a tight leash as Kerslake stood up under a succession of clubbing blows, each of which I expected to finish him. He had been there before and knew what the crowd wanted from him. If he went down too easily it was doubtful he would get another fight. One handed, he attempted to fend off the implacable mutant. By the time he was finally driven to his knees both fighters were covered in Kerslake's free-flowing blood. Standing over the broken form of his vanquished opponent the mutant spat out his gumshield and favoured the crowd with his black smile through a mask of scarlet.

I hustled Brick through the crowd to his stool and checked him out for anything that required prompt attention. Surprisingly, beneath the blood his wounds were entirely superficial. His skin was like rhinoceros hide and appeared to be healing already. The girl began to sponge the gore away from his grinning face. I took a moment to watch Kerslake being dragged from the emptying circle.

"Get the money," I said to Armelle, pushing my way into the crush of bodies surrounding the victor.

It took all my willpower to get outside before the pressure from my stomach forced itself into my throat. I fell onto my knees against the wall to the side of the warehouse's huge sliding doors and vomited steadily until I felt sure that there was nothing left to come but stomach. I rolled onto my back and closed my eyes, oblivious of the pooled vomit beside my head and the feet of the dispersing crowd. I did not want to think, to admit the charge I got out of the butchery back inside. I did not want to admit that I was the same as the punters I had so self-righteously despised.

I had to get away from the mutant, even if it meant losing Armelle. I knew that I was in love with her but it was love that had a hopeless doomed aura about it, the type Russian novelists seem to specialise in. Maybe after the pounding the mutant had taken I could slip his bonding. I tried to force myself upright but failed. My legs felt as though they had just completed a marathon. My arms shook so much I could not even sit up. Whether it was nausea or the mutant's control made no difference. Either way I was still held.

Cool, soft hands lifted my head. A scarf brushed the residue of conscience off my mouth and without looking I knew it was Armelle. I allowed her to rest my head in her lap. For a few short minutes she would be mine alone.

"I collected the money," she said.

They were not the words I wanted to hear.

Following our debut, fights came quickly and easily. The mutant became a better boxer as my control of him improved. We never won easily but we won. The punters loved us. We cleaned out the north-east inside six months and it was time to move on, to move up. The mutant was reluctant to leave the narrow side streets and magpie nest of his old life. I could sympathise. His flat had become home to me and I had begun to feel safe and comforted amidst the flotsam. But if he wanted to fight he knew there was no choice. We spent a couple of months dredging the husk of London, built on our reputation in Manchester and finally headed for the big time in Birmingham. We had contacts, there was no need to go looking for the money men.

The place where it all happened, where deals were made and the odds struck was a club called Rinty's. As always, I took Armelle along as decoration; front is important to these people. The bouncer noted the expensive clothes, Armelle's jewellery, the projector for the cosmetic hologram that disguised my game leg, and passed us through. I winced at the wave of sound that broke over us as the door opened. It was like every other club we had made connections in, only more so. The meat was more frantic; rictus grins failing to disguise their desperation, hardly even fooling themselves. The sharks patrolled ceaselessly, attracted by the thrashing. Sleek and deadly, feeding on pain.

A waitress saw my hunger and directed us towards a table on the fringe of the dance floor. She knew what I was, even if I would not admit to it. I placed a hand on her arm and shook my head. She glanced at the girl, attempting a quick reappraisal, but was disappointed. Armelle did not fit any of the usual templates. She was out of place. There. With me. The calmness of her face and the slow, relaxed way she moved plainly stated that she needed none of this. She was there by choice. She was her own person. By that very fact she elevated me onto the cigars and Scotch plane. A hostess directed us to the VIP lounge.

Eric Hastall considered himself a sporting gentleman. He owned Rinty's and controlled most of the betting action citywide. His cultured accent was not the type that could be learned or implanted, you had to be born with it. Everything about him said old money.

Armelle slipped naturally into the understated elegance of the room but to me the deep pile of the carpet just made balance more difficult. I was wary of the polished wood and leather and crystal surroundings, the hushed atmosphere of people conversing in semi-whispers. She appeared to absorb the ambience, breathe it effortlessly.

On a raised catwalk at waist height around the room, naked figures moved obscenely to background musak. Most were mutilated or mutated in one way or another and in amongst them were patrons in various stages of undress. Armelle gently squeezed my hand; I wrenched my gaze from the sideshow and pulled myself together. Yet again I had reason to wonder at my companion's background.

Hastall snapped his fingers and a waiter swooped with drinks. "Champagne for the lady," our host murmured, serving her himself. "And brandy." He removed the balloons from the tray and handed me one.

I paused, watching him swirl the liquor about the glass and dipping downwards to inhale its bouquet. Attempting to imitate him would have made me look more awkward than I already felt so I contented myself with a conservative flourish of the spirit before attempting a tentative sip.

"You are Lawless, I believe," Hastall said.

I was not overly surprised that he knew who we were. A cripple and a beauty in tandem were difficult to miss. "That's right, Mr Hastall," I said, returning the compliment.

"And your exquisite companion?"

"Armelle."

"Armelle...?" He spoke as though I had been tactless at the very least by making such an informal introduction.

I had never thought to ask her surname. She had never seemed to need more definition than those two flowing syllables.

"Velkinskaya," Armelle supplied. She stared into his eyes as though daring him to intrude further into her privacy. Hastall broke eye contact rapidly though not, I thought, without regret.

"Can we talk?" he said to me.

The next step in the dance. "Armelle is... a partner."

"Ah! Good. I'll come straight to the point," Hastall said. "Without my say so there are no more fights for you and your boy. I wish to purchase a half share in him."

I was surprised and disappointed at the abruptness of his approach. His demand was not unforeseen but I had been expecting something akin to a courtship ritual beforehand. "I don't own Brick," I said, "so there's nothing I can sell."

"I'm not taking a negotiating stance, Mr Lawless, I am stating the facts. I will give you ten thousand credits, which is more than generous, and I'm in for fifty percent. Your relationship with the fighter is of no concern to me."

I hesitated before replying. It was put up or shut up time. The last thing I could afford in this company was to appear powerless. If Brick spoke for himself, what did they need with me? I liked the semblance of partnership in my relationship with the mutant and Armelle; being relegated to hired help did not appeal.

"The price..."

"The price," Hastall interrupted, "is, as I said, generous and also not negotiable."

"When do we get the ten kay?" I said. We could always cut out later.

Hastall smiled and reached inside his jacket. The envelope he passed to me appeared bulky enough to contain the amount but I pointedly tore it open and counted the contents, smiling at Hastall all the while.

"I'll arrange all the details for our man's next contest," Hastall said curtly. "Have him ready to fight in a fortnight." He signalled to a waiter standing just out of earshot. "If you will excuse me I have some other matters to attend to."

The waiter relieved us of our glasses. Now that the transaction was completed our presence was no longer necessary or desirable.

As we turned to go Hastall said to me, "Perhaps Armelle would care to stay on. I'm sure we can come to an arrangement."

I saw his movement in the water, sensed him circling. He attempted to look casual, unconcerned one way or the other, but I knew him now. His appetite was refined, as was the air that he breathed, but beneath the facade he was just another punter. I offered the girl my arm and escorted her from the lounge without replying. The score evened. Self respect is a rare and expensive commodity.

"You want a drink," I shouted over the pounding jagged beat that blanketed us.

Armelle nodded and we eased our way to the bar. She watched the dancers intently as I waited for my order. There was a longing in her that I had not seen before. Her body moved, involuntarily drawing truncated designs with hands, feet and head.

I nudged her with my elbow. "Go on, if you want."

"You?" she mouthed across the noise.

I shrugged and jabbed a finger at my leg. The hologram didn't help me walk. Her head bobbed understanding in time to the music. She moved in a dancing glide to the drug dispensers and bought herself a short-burning cocktail. High stepping backwards onto the dance floor she smiled at me through a cascade of hair as her neck loosened and her limbs took on the semblance of discrete intelligences.

The screens loved her, picking up her rhythm and flashing her across the walls in ten foot splendour. The camera jock was an artist, accentuating the length of her legs, the curves and planes of her face with low angles. For an hour she was his star as she strobed across the screens, filling them with her energy and animal heat. This surely was the real Armelle, not the shadow created by the mutant for his own enjoyment. I longed to free her, to release her into the world where she could swim freely, confounding the sharks with the certainty of her strokes. I longed to love her to the final breath of my life.

Hastall controlled every aspect of fist fighting in Birmingham except one: Wulf Tanner. I had seen Tanner in the old days when it was boxing and they used gloves, fighting in a square ring with rules and judges; when losers didn't always leave on a stretcher. He was young and raw then but he exuded class. From what I heard he still did. And Tanner was his own man; nobody owned him or any piece of him. What Eric Hastall could not own he would destroy. Brick was to be the instrument of that destruction.

It felt like old times. Hastall erected a ring in the cavernous, vaulted cellar of his club, built tiers of seating around it and put up huge video screens so that every move could be savoured, every cut pored over and every weakness devoured. The old round system would be in operation, though of six minutes duration rather than three. He even suggested that gloves be worn but the audience would never have stood for that; even for a bout that was being billed as the World Heavyweight Championship. Considering the hype surrounding the match, Hastall must have paid off the police forces of at least three counties as well as senior junta officials.

As challengers, we were first into the ring. The mutant sat in his corner as though it was just another cash gig in just another backstreet, hating the twisted faces equally whether they yelled insults or encouragement. Armelle stood on the apron of the ring massaging his shoulders and murmuring soothing words.

A fanfare announced the arrival of the Champ. The mutant did not even bother looking up and the girl never missed a beat with her hands or her litany of ease. But I could not keep my gaze away from Tanner. He was magnificent. Only slightly taller than the mutant, but built in perfect proportion. His head was shaven and his skin shone like oiled obsidian. As he approached the ring I could see only faint evidence of his age – by my calculations he was in his late thirties at least – and not a single mark or blemish on his skin. I could not be sure which I feared most: defeat or watching the perfection of Tanner crushed by the pitiless onslaught of the mutant.

Wulf Tanner milked the crowd in the lead-up to the bell. The mutant bit down on his gumshield with the remaining shards of his diseased teeth, loathing his opponent no more than anyone else.

For the first two rounds the fight followed a familiar pattern. Tanner hit the mutant with everything in his armoury, taking little in return. Brick moved forward slowly, one-paced, throwing few punches, conserving energy and keeping his chin tucked in. Between rounds Armelle massaged and murmured; there was little for me to do except wet him down and clean his gumshield. There were never any cuts to treat.

Although the formal ring gave him no problems, the breaks every six minutes seemed to kill the mutant's rhythm and it was only in the second half of the rounds that he was finding his opponent's range. Tanner respected the mutant's power and as the fight progressed began to pick his punches more carefully. There was no way he was prepared to take a punch in order to land one. The mutant had to earn every opening and by the eighth round I was convinced the price was too high.

Eric Hastall came to the same conclusion. During the ninth he made his way down to ringside. I could hear him screaming in my ear but I had a full plate keeping the mutant's face and Tanner's fists separate. When the bell sounded at the end of the round I relaxed and stepped back from the apron. I needed a rest as much as Brick. For the past three rounds Armelle had handled the corner work alone.

Hastall was still yelling at me above the rumble of the crowd. "... out of his head. I've been watching you, you're not his fucking trainer, you

143

fancy yourself as some type of puppeteer. You needed a body so you've taken his. You're riding him out there. It's you that's dictating his moves. It's you that's losing him this fight."

"He wouldn't have lasted half an hour without me. He'd have worn himself out swinging away at nothing."

Hastall's lips were drawn back past his teeth to reveal his gums. He looked like a tiger shark in a feeding frenzy. "Get out of his head you fucking mutant. Without you he can win this."

I laughed in his face. Hastall was having difficulty keeping his hands away from my throat.

Armelle knelt on the canvas and bent her head close to Hastall's. "Matthew is not a mutant, Mr Hastall."

He looked from the girl to me and then to Brick. The mutant turned slowly on his stool and presented him with a bruised smile. The bell sounded and Armelle fumbled Brick's gumshield back into his mouth, patting his shoulder. The mutant stood up unconcerned, as though he was going to the bar to buy a round of drinks. He strode purposefully toward the centre of the ring, his chin tucked neatly against his shoulder and brought his hands up in the classic defensive posture. Tanner waded in as he did at the beginning of every round. Hastall continued screaming abuse at me, occasionally shouting at our fighter. Now that I knew the theme some of it managed to force its way into my consciousness.

"Let him go, Brick," I heard amidst the obscenities.

Tanner had been concentrating on the mutant's body since round five. Brick's breathing was becoming laboured.

"Cut him loose," Hastall yelled. "You can take Tanner without him."

The mutant's forward progress faltered under a welter of stinging punches. I could feel doubt tensing his muscles. For once I was glad of the bell.

Hastall pushed me away from the corner and climbed onto the apron. "You're losing," he screamed. "You're going to lose. Whatever Lawless did for you in the past, it's no good now."

The mutant's head turned slowly to face Hastall. "I need him. He's mine." His expression and the words did not quite match.

One minute and fourteen seconds into round eleven Tanner caught the mutant with a vicious overarm swing that took him high on the side of the head. His knees buckled and he crumpled to the canvas taking three wicked blows to the back of the neck as he fell. We had one minute to get him back on his feet. I contemplated holding him under. Bonded, it might just be possible.

With Armelle's help I managed to drag Brick back to his corner. A glance at the timekeeper told me it would be a long minute. The mutant's bandaged hand closed on my wrist. His eyes were clear. Frightened and sad. A feeling of nausea mushroomed in my stomach. There was a brief searing flash of pain behind my eyes as though a white hot needle had been pushed into my head and instantly withdrawn.

"I've got to do this by myself," he said.

"No, Brick..."

I wanted to vomit. I wanted to scream but was afraid of the echoing emptiness inside my skull that I had never felt before. I wanted to run; never to stop running; never to look back.

He squeezed my wrist convulsively, grinding his teeth together. "It's done. Leave me."

I was myself again. Alone. I felt used and hurt and unclean but I was free. My thoughts were a confused tangle, toppling one into the other without any clear sense of priority.

The timekeeper rang his bell. "Seconds out."

Brick pushed himself off the canvas and climbed to his feet without apparent ill effects from the knock down. Armelle tugged at my sleeve pulling me from the ring. Tanner resumed his onslaught. Hastall, from my former place at ringside, yelled encouragement at the mutant.

I turned from the fight and swung the girl to face me. "He couldn't have freed me without unbonding you as well." I took a deep breath as my heart tried to push itself into my mouth. "Come with me. Now."

She looked at me calmly, brushing a strand of hair away from her eyes. "I was never bonded to Brick," she said. "Not in that way."

"I... I thought..."

"I know. Don't say any more, Matt." She half turned back towards the ring. "You should go."

It was as though with those words my life had ended. Now I was truly empty. I looked past her to the fight. Tanner was moving in to finish it. The mutant had his head covered by his hands as blow after blow hammered into his unprotected ribs. I told myself there was nothing I could have done. An arm's length away Hastall screamed advice and invective. The mutant bent over as though to present a reduced target to his persecutor. Tanner closed, holding Brick's head with one hand and driving the other fist repeatedly into the area behind his seemingly defenceless adversary's ear. A cry of rage, pain and intense hatred was wrenched from the mutant's swollen lips, the first sound I had heard him make in the course of a fight.

Brick, right hand leaning on one bent knee, jack-knifed upright pushing Tanner clear with the other arm. The move took Tanner completely by surprise, propelling him sharply backwards into the ropes. The mutant straightened and drew back his right as Tanner was catapulted back towards him off balance. Legs planted like Doric columns, Brick threw a straight right that had every ounce of his strength and hostility behind it and Tanner stumbled helplessly into it, head up.

Once, on my grandfather's farm when I was a child, I saw a heavy plank fall lengthwise onto a chicken, squashing it flat. The noise it made was the closest thing I have heard to the sound of that punch landing. Tanner went completely limp as though all the bones in his body had dissolved, but he remained upright. The crowd noise changed from pandemonium to absolute silence in an instant.

The impact of the mutant's punch had driven Tanner's left cheekbone back into his skull leaving a dark, welling cavity that swallowed one side of his nose and an eye. The remaining eye was wide, as though he had just remembered something terribly important. The mutant stood perfectly still. The only sound was the scrape of Tanner's boot on the canvas as he slowly pivoted on one leg like a drunken ballerina in a music box. The back of his head had ruptured in a jagged vertical line and a ledge of bone showed clearly through the dark ooze.

It was as though my mind was overloaded. The pictures it received were failing to make coherent sense so it retreated, allowing only brief images through into its secret place. My eyes focused on the swell of avid faces squeezing the final droplets of suffering from Tanner's upright corpse. Whatever I thought I had been at my lowest ebb, it was never one of them.

Like a video camera my vision tracked backwards into the ring as Tanner's body realised it was dead and finally heeled over onto the canvas to lie like a heap of unconnected parts. The mutant stood immobile and I was glad his face was turned away from me. The hunched shoulders and loose hanging arms swaying almost imperceptibly, in time to the beat of his heart. It is an image of desolation that will never leave me.

The hungry eyes looked away. Sated. Until next time.

Love Song

Outsiders seldom came to the village, set as it was way back in the wilds of the mountains. So visitors always caused a stir. Philip Arnesti was not only an outsider, he was also a foreigner. An American and, therefore, exotic. A graduate student, his visit centred around his thesis. Indeed, his research in the village could provide the heart of the document.

He arrived by car towards the middle of an autumn afternoon. Already the skies were darkening, pulling grey clouds about them like God's eiderdown. Even in the waning light, his vehicle appeared shiny and alien.

Philip himself looked like a big game hunter who had taken a wrong turning somewhere east of Java. Khaki chinos and an olive jacket festooned with large patch pockets. Rangy, athletic body. Piercing blue eyes behind black Wayfarer sunglasses.

He opened the boot of the car. A sticker in the back window proclaimed its owners to be a hire firm in Tralee. Bags piled up at his feet. He draped an expensive Canon single lens reflex camera around his neck; the sort of instrument professionals carried. A large black and yellow camera bag with Kodak emblazoned across the sides was slung casually across his shoulder. By the time he closed the boot lid there were too many individual items for him to carry unaided.

A crowd of small boys, like mongrel ducks, had gathered a dozen yards away, near the door of Glennon's pub. It had to be his destination.

Nowhere else in the village offered overnight accommodation. Even in the season seldom more than a handful of tourists made it this far off the commercially beaten track. Few of them stayed for longer than it took to eat lunch or drink a pint of Guinness.

Philip paused with his hand still pressing on the boot lid, as out of place on this narrow street as a penguin in Death Valley. He stared at the gathered children. They returned his stare. Their faces betrayed no opinion or judgement of him. Their presence the only indication of curiosity.

Slowly, Philip raised the camera to his eye. The model had autofocus which was just as well; Philip was no photographer. The camera had been loaned to him by his professor to help document background detail. The youngsters didn't strictly qualify, but his instincts told him to get the snap anyway. He had loaded a fast black and white film on recommendation and had been told that all remained for him was to point and shoot.

He imagined the photograph appearing in *The New Yorker* or *Life*, whoever published that sort of thing these days. The boys had that unaffected, urchin look; an image from a past that never was. He wondered how much of the pub window was in the frame. Philip refocused and took a second shot. The children were not as well centred but the background was better established. Mentally, he shrugged and allowed the camera to return to its hanging position against his sternum.

The pub door opened and a short, plump man with a florid complexion and thinning sandy hair stepped into the street. He glanced from Philip to the group of boys, then back to Philip. "Hello," he said. "Will you want a room?"

"Yes," Philip said. "Please," he added after a moment's hesitation.

The florid man turned slightly towards the youngsters. "Give the man a hand, then." To Philip he said, "Come on inside. You'll be wanting a drink after your journey."

There didn't seem to be a way for Philip to refuse. He picked up the Kodak bag and left the others to the boys.

Philip had a pint of warm bottled Guinness, a shower, and afterwards dined with the Glennon family. There were no restaurants in the village and the three pubs, Glennon's included, served only sandwiches, and then only at lunchtime.

The florid man was Mr Glennon who turned out to have the answers to more questions about the village and its history than Philip knew to ask.

"I'm hoping to speak to a man called Colm Og O'Riordan," Philip said, as they drank strong, black tea after their meal.

"For the stories," Mrs Glennon said.

Philip nodded.

He had already spent two summers in the Appalachians persuading people to allow him record their folk tales and songs. In his heart he felt he had an adequate thesis in those tapes. If there was anything here like the wealth of songs and stories he had discovered in Scotland in the past week, there was also a book, if he could do justice to the material. And Colm Og O'Riordan was reputed to have the greatest store of Celtic folklore, poetry and songs left in the world. The cross references in the Scottish material was indisputable. The Irish stuff would be better. He just knew it.

Mr Glennon packed a pipe contemplatively while his wife cleared the table. He pressed the tobacco deep into the blackened bowl with a callused thumb and added a few more shreds of the rich, aromatic mixture. "I'll take you to him in the morning."

"That's very kind, but there's no need."

Glennon drew out his matches from the pocket of his waistcoat and struck one. He held it up as though critically judging the quality of the flame. Philip waited, holding his breath, as the burnt, blackened end of the match began to curl. Finally his landlord applied the yellow flame to the tobacco and drew on it. The resulting smoke had little of the wonderful aroma of the raw tobacco. Glennon puffed up a grey screen between them then waited while it settled into a flat, thin cloud just above head height. "He's not a well man."

"I can wait until he's better, I guess. I have a week, maybe more."

Glennon shook his head. "He's dying."

The words knocked the wind out of him. It took a few moments to regain his equilibrium. Without O'Riordan he could still have a thesis and defend it; there were other Irish poets and storytellers. But the book would be unlikely.

Glennon produced more clouds of smoke and watched him, like a predator staking out a watering hole. One thing the past couple of years of research had taught the young American was when and how to remain silent. Glennon smoked for ten minutes then pushed himself out of his chair. "Time I made an appearance in the bar," he said. At the kitchen door he stopped. "We'll have breakfast at eight, then I can get you up to Colm Og without ruining my morning."

"Thank you," Philip said to the closing door. It had been a long day and he was too tired to satisfy the curiosity of the locals. Bed seemed a far more pleasant option than the bar.

Colm Og O'Riordan's dwelling was a tiny, slate roofed cottage set hard against a narrow twisting ribbon of tarmac. Philip was forced to drive fifty yards past in order to park his hire car in a field gateway. Somewhere inland, the sun had risen dispersing the thin early mist. As shafts of sunlight broke over the treeline, the grass displayed its shining dewy ornamentation, like diamonds set in silver. Downslope to the west, the village huddled in shadow.

Though all about him was picture postcard scenery, it was the silence that impressed Philip. Apart from the footsteps of Glennon and himself, he could hear nothing else. No breeze disturbed the trees. No birds sang. No insects buzzed. Having lived in cities all his life Philip had never experienced a pure absence of noise. He placed his hand on Glennon's arm. They stopped. He listened intently. There was nothing. He could not suppress a smile.

Their knock at the cottage door was answered by a slight, female figure barely out of her teens. Her right hand brushed hair clear of her eyes. She nodded. "Mr Glennon. How are you, this morning?"

"Fine, Noreen, thanks. How's your Da."

"Ask him yourself. I wouldn't deny him the pleasure of enumerating his symptoms for a fresh audience."

Glennon laughed. "I won't be coming in thanks, Noreen, but," he indicated Philip with a sweep of his hand, "this gentleman has come all the way from America to talk to him, if that's possible."

Noreen turned her attention to the stranger at the publican's side. He smiled and took a step forward, thrusting out a hand for her to shake.

"Philip Arnesti. Pleased to meet you," he said.

Noreen shook his hand tentatively.

"I'm hoping to talk to your father about his songs and stories, maybe record a couple." He patted the Walkman Pro on his belt.

Noreen thought it made him look like a gunslinger from the Hollywood westerns her father had been so fond of when she was younger. When he had been healthy enough for the trip into Tralee just to see a film.

"If it's not too much of an imposition," Philip added. "Mr Glennon told me he was ill."

"An audience is never an imposition for my father."

Glennon said, "I'll leave you to it, Philip. The Beamish rep is due to call this morning. He said he'll be early and I'd hate to miss him."

Philip regretted his decision to drive up here. Had they walked he would not feel awkward about not offering Glennon a lift back to the village.

Noreen disappeared through the low front door of the cottage. He ducked his head under the lintel as he followed. The room he entered appeared to take up three quarters of the floor space of the structure. It was stone floored and cluttered with furniture that looked to have been hand made, probably from oak and a long time ago. A table stood centre stage. One end was covered with sewing materials; at the other a single place was set for breakfast. Two huge rocking chairs sat in front of a fireplace big enough to walk into. Philip guessed that the household's cooking had been done there within the last generation.

"Come on," Noreen said, leading him towards a door at the rear of the room, "I'll take you through to Colm Og."

"Don't you want to check it's okay with him, first?"

"He'd have my life if he thought I let you get away."

The door gave onto a room barely big enough to hold a narrow single bed. A man with a face brown and wrinkled as old leather sat in the bed, propped up by numerous pillows. The leather skin hung loosely on the bones of his skull and sagged on his forearms. It was as though his skeleton had shrunk beneath his flesh. He could never have been a big man, but now he seemed birdlike and would have appeared insignificant if not for the strength of his nose and chin, or the fire in eyes which burned fiercely beneath brows that remained thick and black.

"This is Philip Arnesti," Noreen said. "He's an American."

Philip was unsure whether the last was explanation or excuse. The old man stared intently at him, his head moving slowly as his eyes travelled the contours of his visitor's face. He grunted, as though in assent. "You've come to listen."

"Yes, sir."

"Sir," Colm Og said. "I like that." To Noreen he said, "An extraordinarily polite race the Americans, full of please and thank you and sir and ma'am. We could learn a lot from them." His eyes and attention returned to Philip. "I travelled to America once, you know."

"Did you like it?"

"Not enough to stay." Colm Og chuckled deep in his chest. The chuckle mutated instantly into a cough which left him bent double and gasping for breath. Noreen stepped close in and supported his shoulders. When the coughing fit subsided she helped him upright. As his breathing returned to normal he patted the girl's hand. "We could learn a thing or two from the Americans," he said.

Noreen smiled fondly at him. "Yes father."

"They have great waiters."

"I know, father."

He coughed again, but this time it did not appear life threatening. "I was talking to Philip."

"I'm sure Philip knows far more about service in American restaurants than we ever will," she said.

He patted her hand once more. "You're right, Noreen love. As usual." He let go her hand and heaved himself further upright. "Now take Philip inside and give him a cup of tea. I'll be there in a minute."

"Are you sure you should?" Noreen said, an edge of concern in her voice.

"I need my hearth for the telling."

While the old man readied himself, Noreen prepared the main room. She set the fire; raking ashes and building a square of peat briquettes around a white, paraffin soaked firelighter. Across the top of the edifice she strategically placed lumps of coal, then applied a match to the firelighter.

Colm Og's rocker was set at the left of the fireplace. The angle and the placing appeared exact. The cushions were distributed as though by a mathematical formula. Noreen stood back to examine her work, made a minute adjustment before heading for the kitchen. "Pull up the other chair," she said.

Philip sat down opposite the dressed rocker and waited for the ancient poet. Noreen returned shortly with tea. One-handed, she swung a straight backed kitchen chair close to Colm Og's rocker. "You'll need to sit a bit closer. His voice doesn't carry the way it used." She set the mugs of tea on the seat of the kitchen chair.

Colm Og appeared wearing a suit over a white shirt open at the neck. The suit's cut was Seventies, with wide lapels plunging deep to button around about his navel. Philip doubted it had ever suited the old man. Possibly it was a cast off, though it fit well enough, allowing for the amount of weight he had lost to illness.

The walk from the door to his chair was measured and seemed to cost much of his energy reserve. Noreen helped him into the rocker. He sat for a couple of minutes concentrating on breathing evenly. After the first minute he cast a reassuring smile that was mostly grimace at Philip.

Once recovered, he attacked the tea with gusto. "There's a story about a Spanish sea captain from Dingle, you might like. Or perhaps you would prefer a song to start."

"If we have time I would like to hear a little of everything. Poetry, stories and songs."

"I have nothing left but time," the old man said. "And none too much of that. But what I have I will gladly share with you."

Philip produced his Walkman, holding it up for his host to see. "Do you mind?"

Colm Og glanced to his daughter. Noreen said, "It's an oral tradition. People are expected to listen carefully and remember. They retell the story, sometimes changing a word or two. It makes the stories grow. Keeps them alive."

"But what about the poems and songs? You need to get the words right."

Colm Og nodded. "Those you learn by heart. I myself know a fair number."

"How many, roughly. A hundred. Five hundred."

The old man smiled. "Two maybe three thousand poems. A few more songs. I find the songs easier. Always did. The tunes help with the memory."

"Two or three thousand?" Philip found it impossible to keep his voice free of incredulity.

"I've forgotten many."

"But thousands." He shook his head.

"I've spent a lifetime storing them up. Not everyone can do it. Some remember a little. Some a lot."

"Some nothing at all," Noreen added pointedly.

"I'm a student, not a poet," Philip said. "If I'm to do justice to your store of songs and folktales I need to use the machine."

"This is for school? For learning?" Colm Og asked.

"Yes."

He sat back into his rocker and set it into motion. It rumbled gently against the uneven surface of the floor. He stared into the fire as though searching for the answer in the flames. After a while he stopped rocking and sat forward. "Turn it on."

Noreen cleared the mugs off the chair seat, leaving it for the tape recorder. Philip pressed the record button and placed it close to the old man. Colm Og cleared his throat and sat forward so that his mouth was next to the machine.

"That's not necessary," Philip said. "It's got good pickup. Just get comfortable."

"Right." Colm Og sat upright. He focused on a point above Philip's head and began. "*Nuair a chuaigh Aoingeas MacGloinn go dthi Baile na Droichead Briste...*"

"I'm sorry," Philip interrupted, "but I don't speak Gaelic." He smiled apologetically. "Could you do it in English?"

Colm Og's ancient brow furrowed. It was difficult to identify the new wrinkles. "They can only be told as I heard them. The language is a vital part of the tale. Changing the language changes the words which changes the story itself."

Noreen returned from the kitchen. She pulled up a stool and sat beside her father, leaning her forearm on the arm of his chair and laying her chin on that. It was a curiously childlike pose.

Colm Og placed his hand on top of the girl's. "If you wish to turn off the device I will gladly give you the sense of the story."

"It's not the sense of the story I want, it's the story itself, as it has been remembered and handed down."

"Yes. But that is in the Irish. I can only be true to the tale in the language of its birth and mine."

"Tell the story father. Talk to the machine. It cares not whether it is English or Irish you speak." She sat straight, her arm still resting on the arm of the rocker. "Afterwards we'll take the tape and I will translate it for you. Will that do?"

Philip was not keen on the solution but he doubted it was possible to persuade the old man to change his mind. The girl's offer looked like the only way he was going to get anything useful out of O'Riordan. "Thank you, Noreen. I would be most grateful for your help."

"Good," said Colm Og. "That's decided then. If your machine's ready...?"

Philip rewound the tape to the beginning and reset it to record.

"Nuair a chuaigh Aoingeas MacGloinn go dthi Baile na Droichead Briste..."

Colm Og began again.

Though he could understand not a word of what the storyteller was saying, Philip found himself hooked by the subtle rhythms and cadences of the language and the speaker's voice. The old man told the story directly to him as though he spoke fluent Irish and comprehended every nuance of the delivery. At the end Colm Og flopped back into his chair, drained.

Noreen stood. "I'll make some lunch."

Philip suggested he could drive back to Glennon's pub and grab a bite there. She would hear none of it. He was their guest. Lunch consisted of a thin chicken broth accompanied by as much home-baked bread as could be wished for. When it was finished Noreen offered to help her father back to his room. He declined. It was a while since he had sat before his own hearth and he intended to see out the day there.

Noreen and Philip sat at the table and she translated the words on the tape while he scribbled them down into a soft covered notebook. He regretted leaving his laptop back at the pub. It had made sense at the time. The plan had been to transcribe the tapes in the evening. But that was before the language problem arose.

By the time the tapes were transcribed Philip's hand was cramping regularly. It was dark outside. The old man was asleep in his chair. "I've taken up your entire day," Philip said.

"My days revolve around Colm Og," Noreen said. "Today was a good one. He hasn't had many of late. He has few enough left to him."

"Would he be up to doing this again tomorrow?"

Noreen shrugged. "He might not live until tomorrow. But I think he will if he knows you'll be back."

Philip said nothing. His face posed the question.

"It's a long time since anyone asked to hear his stories. They have the television now. What do they need with an old man who uses only Irish. Half of them don't speak it themselves."

"I see."

"If the old ones spare him, he would love to see you again tomorrow."

"The old ones?"

She smiled. "The old gods who ruled when people like Colm Og were respected, important members of the community. The ones who were here before St Patrick." Her smile broadened. "Who still might be here if only someone would believe in them."

"Do you?" he asked.

She laughed. It was the first time Philip noticed her as a separate being rather than an extension of the old man. She was not a classical beauty by any means but her thick red hair bounced on her shoulders with a vitality of its own, matched by the spark in her eyes which added a glint of fey wickedness to her laughing mouth. "I'm part of the MTV generation. Or I would be if I could persuade Colm Og to have a television set in the house. I lived in Cork city for a year after I left school. Before I had to come home and look after himself."

"That must have been hard."

"Not at all. I love my father. I would not have missed the opportunity to be with him now for all the Guinness in St James's Gate Brewery." She laughed, then added in a serous tone, "I often wish he had been younger when I was born so that I could have had more time with him. But I'll make the most of what I have."

*

The following morning Philip made his way back up the mountain to Colm Og's cottage. The old man was already sitting by the fire when he arrived. Philip was surprised at how fresh he looked.

The old man had decided they should turn their attention to poetry. "Perhaps you might even learn a few stanzas," he said.

Philip grinned and set out his tape machine. Beside it he placed a stack of four cassettes. Noreen pulled up her stool. "You'll be working him hard then."

"Both of you," Philip said. He was pleased by the smile with which she rewarded him. The shiver it sent along his spine was a surprise. It almost caused him to miss the start of Colm Og's recitation. The old man pressed the record button.

As Colm Og spoke his poetry in the incomprehensible tongue of his ancestors, Philip found himself watching the girl. Mostly her eyes were on her father or the licking flames of the fire. Only occasionally did she glance in Philip's direction. He began to spend the intervals between those glances in anticipation of the next one. He wished they would linger a while, seek communication, pass secret, silent messages as the music of Colm Og's voice lulled his senses.

They broke at lunch time, and in the afternoon again translated the morning's work while the old man slept before his hearth. This time he had his laptop. The ache when he finished was in his back. And maybe stirring in his heart.

The following day Philip suggested that as they had already dipped into Colm Og's store of poetry and stories, the time might be right for song.

Colm Og shook his head. "In my time I could sing. My voice was adequate. There were some who told me that with training it could have been something to hear. But I had not the time. Now, I have not the voice."

"Quality's not important."

"Singing is beyond me," Colm Og said. "Entirely."

"Oh." The sound was hollow with disappointment.

The old man smiled. "Noreen is a better singer than I ever dreamed of being."

Noreen blushed, directing her eyes towards the floor. "Father."

"'Tis but the truth. Nothing else." He patted her hand. "I have taught her many from my store of songs. Enough to fill all the tapes you could buy."

"Will you sing for me, Noreen?" Philip asked.

She looked up into his eyes. At last a secret message passed between them. It told him that whatever she sang would be for him.

Colm Og squeezed his daughter's hand and spoke a few brief words to her in Irish. It sounded to Philip like a song title. The girl nodded, shook her hair away from her face and, tilting it slightly upward, began to sing. Her voice was high and pure and sweet but with a promise of power beneath, should it be required. Each note was reached effortlessly and Philip could detect no flaw in her pitch or any element of her delivery. In song, her face was transformed into real beauty.

After a dozen songs, each prompted by her father, Noreen shook her head. "I will choose," she said simply.

"Of course," Colm Og said. "It is your right."

Although he did not understand the words, Philip felt the meaning of the new songs in his guts. They were songs of love and desire. They were songs to bind a man to a woman. When she was finished, Noreen stood abruptly and went to the kitchen. Philip remained in his seat. He felt tired, as though he had been supporting an enormous weight for the space of the morning.

"It is a fine thing to hear such songs sung by one with the voice," Colm Og said. He sat with his face turned towards the fire, his eyes closed.

"The voice?" Philip asked.

"It is a quality that such singing possesses," the old man said. "Hereabouts, in my day they called it *the* voice."

Philip thought about it. "Sort of magical."

"It has magic, yes."

"The magic of the old ones?"

Colm Og's head snapped around to stare at him, eyes hard and flat like shards of flint. "What do you know of the old ones?"

"Nothing. Noreen mentioned the name yesterday, that's all."

"What did she say?"

Noreen spoke from the kitchen door. "I referred to them jokingly. As did Philip."

"They're not a matter for jest."

In the afternoon as Noreen translated the words of her own songs, Philip found himself watching her every move intently as he typed. When she spoke he stared into her face, observing the way her lips formed the words, the way her fingers worried at the nimbus of fine hair in her fringe which refused to go with the tide swept back behind an ear.

He listened intently not only to her words but to the soft timbre of her voice. He was aware of the sound of her clothing as it adjusted to her smallest movement. He knew when she crossed her ankles or shifted a foot across the floor. He saw and heard every breath. He could not be certain whether any of what she said ended up on disc. His fingers might have been typing anything. His eyes never thought to seek confirmation.

On his way out Philip once more arranged to call the following day. As he walked slowly to his car the cold evening air cleared his head. He had two days remaining before he must begin his journey home to Iowa. There was a poet in Mayo he needed to interview. He could not afford to spend another day with Colm Og O'Riordan and his wonderful daughter. He had all he needed from them.

That thought stopped him cold. He backed up to *wonderful daughter*. On the first visit he had hardly noticed Noreen as a woman. On the second she made a profound impact on him. Today, she had fascinated him completely. As if she had woven a spell.

His attraction to Noreen was a matter of chemistry, he told himself, added to the fact that he had not been on a date in six weeks. Not surprisingly his hormones had begun to act up.

Philip retraced his steps back to the house. Noreen was surprised when she opened the door. He explained that he had forgotten he had to drive north to Mayo the next day.

"I thought..." She blushed. The heightened colour in her cheeks gave her the look of an adolescent angel.

Philip's arms wanted to hold her. His heart quickened in agreement. The only organ which dissented was his brain. It knew the situation was impossible. He had a thesis to write, a career to pursue, a dream to live of achievement and riches and fame. This girl had no place in it. The person he had been for the past weeks had no place there either. The person he really was had no place in Noreen's life. She would hate the real him. His American dreams.

"I thought there was something," she said. "Between us."

"I have to go to Mayo."

"You could come back."

He shook his head. "I'm sorry." It was true and it was a lie. Every part of him was sorry except that which formed and spoke the words. Had his body been a democracy it would have stayed. He turned reluctantly and went to the car. He could feel her watching all the way.

When the car refused to start a part of him wondered if she had worked some kind of magic on the vehicle. The rational part of his mind slapped it down. To get to the village he had to walk past the cottage. The door was closed, which was a relief. The walk took twenty minutes. When he got there the time was six forty-two. Clancy's shop, which boasted petrol pumps and the town's only auto mechanic, had been shut since six. In a village like this that was unimportant. He knocked on the front door and within ten minutes was on his way back to his car in the passenger seat of the proprietor's van.

They pulled up behind the hire car and climbed out. Mr Clancy was armed with a powerful torch and a heavy blue tin box of tools, covered in oily fingermarks. As the mechanic opened up the bonnet and clipped his torch overhead, Philip wondered should he call at the cottage. It would be rude not to, he thought, but on the other hand it would be awkward for all concerned if he did.

A light moving through the trees above the cottage like a will o' the wisp caught his attention as it bobbled and dipped and disappeared behind tree trunks to reappear higher on the dark mountainside. A prolonged flash of light revealed a pale face. It was Noreen's. He watched intently. Finally the light stopped moving. Behind him the clank of Clancy's tools against the engine block were accompanied by the occasional muttered curse. Here, he would only be in the way.

Philip climbed the gate before which the car was parked and began to walk across the field. A gust of wind ruffled his hair. It carried the plaintive sound of a single voice singing. It was unmistakably Noreen. He stopped and listened hard. The song seemed wordless but he guessed that was because of the intervening distance. He began walking towards the light again, faster.

Soon the song was audible over the sound of his breathing. It was a marvellous sound. He was as entranced as any sailor hearing the sirens. He wanted to stop and listen properly but more, he wanted to be close so that he could look upon the singer as she made her haunting song.

Seamlessly the priority changed from the song to the singer. He began to trot. How could he have been so foolish? Philip asked himself. How could he live, knowing that that voice existed and was denied him? How could he have considered allowing Noreen escape him?

By the time he reached the light he was too breathless to speak. Noreen was sitting on a tree stump. She looked at him and stopped singing. She stared at him while he stood, hands on knees, regaining his breath. "Don't stop," he gasped.

"The song is finished."

He straightened and took a deep breath. He smiled. "I'm not leaving."

"Why?"

It was a question which he hadn't considered. When he did, the answer was simple. "Because I can't. Not without you."

"And I won't leave. Colm Og needs me."

"When he's... when he's gone?"

"Then I will leave," she said.

"With me?"

"With you."

"Can I stay here with you until then?" he asked.

"Yes."

He stepped close and held out his hand to help her to her feet. She took the hand and stood into his embrace. When their first kiss ended Philip knew he had made the best move of his life. "Sing the song again," he whispered. "The one that called me to you."

"I can't."

"Why?"

"I just can't, that's all."

He stepped back to arms length, holding her by the shoulders. "No secrets. Ever," he said.

"The song was for the old ones."

"Go on."

"I sang my love for you."

"And..."

"And made a bargain."

"What bargain?"

"I promised that if they would send you to me I would give them the most valuable gift I had."

"What did you promise them?"

"The voice."

"The voice?" he repeated.

"I promised I would never sing again."

Arguments sprang to his lips. The old ones did not exist. There was no such thing as magic. But his voice would not speak the words. The situation contradicted them. He was there with her. He was going to stay. It did not make sense but it was the way things were. Maybe sometime she would forget her promise. After Colm Og was gone. After they left the mountain. The country. Someday she would again sing her love song for him.

Alias Morton Pinkney

25th July 2153

The body on the slab was a perfect reproduction. Not even his mother would have been able to tell it from the original. Except that it was dead. The original soon would be also. Then, not even the closest scientific inspection could tell that it was only a replica.

All the preparations had been made and the team dispatched. The time shot itself was consuming over eighty percent of their funding, which would leave them only a matter of months to work with the subject. It would have to do. As director of the programme Alan Krause had final responsibility for each project. This one was a unique opportunity to investigate a cultural phenomenon. The subject had not been the one he favoured but even the director wielded only one vote on the committee. He wondered if it would have been possible to push just a little harder for extra funding. Had it been his particular choice of subject, was there another yard he could have gone?

The question was academic now. The operation was beyond the failsafe position. Project Morton Pinkney would be carried through to its logical end. Krause's stomach churned with equal parts of excitement and anxiety. It was the first time two men had been sent back at once. The power drain had been incredible. In less than an hour the system would be recharged and the second shot and pickup made.

Theoretically there should be no problem with the extra weight. But he was a big man and they had never attempted to move so much mass.

16th August 1977

The bedroom stank. A half-consumed hamburger sat on the bedside locker, strands of lettuce curling brokenly from the sides. The only light came from the open door to the bathroom. Derek Mills prevented himself from gagging with difficulty. His partner, Farrell, held a handkerchief up to his nose. Derek wished he had thought of that himself.

The subject lay on the bed semi-comatose. Although he had been intellectually prepared for the subject's condition, the actuality of it splashed into his face like a glass of ice water. For a moment he wondered if they had arrived too late. This body had the bloated, slack appearance of a corpse. Then the head flopped to one side and a low groan escaped the open mouth.

Farrell was all efficiency. From the side pocket of his suit he pulled a slender white tube. He popped off the lid and stowed it carefully back in the pocket, then slid out a hypodermic and the tube followed its cap to rest. Three strides took him to the bedside. Derek knew his job. He stepped alongside and rolled up the left sleeve. Farrell found a vein and slid the needle home, pumping fourteen cc's of go-juice into the subject. They stood back and counted down from thirty.

The subject shuddered and rolled onto his side. His eyes shuttered open. For a moment they were blank, like TV screens before the power is connected. He blinked repeatedly, staring at the intruders in his most private of sanctums. His hand crashed towards the locker, knocking the hamburger to the floor. He scrabbled a drawer open. Derek moved rapidly to intercept the move beating him to the concealed gun with ease.

"Relax, Mr Presley," Farrell said. "We're here to help you."

Derek placed the gun on the floor and slid it under the bed with the side of his foot. Strapped to his back was a long black vinyl tube. He ducked the strap around his head and opened it.

Elvis sat up on the bed, moving with difficulty like a beached manatee. His eyes flickered nervously about the room. His mouth opened and his throat worked but no sound emerged. His hand shot to his throat as though searching for a wound. The eyes filled with terror. The sluggish body failed to respond with the requisite energy to the escape impulses transmitted by a drug fogged brain.

"We gave you a shot to wake you up, Mr Presley," Farrell said. "Something of a cocktail, but that will be nothing new to you." He smiled. "One portion of it was a temporary vocal inhibitor. That will take about ten minutes to wear off. In the interim I suggest you listen to what my colleague, Mr Mills, has to say."

Elvis looked slowly round at Derek. His mouth worked. He gestured for a drink. Farrell went to the bathroom and filled a glass with water. Elvis drank greedily, splashing a quarter of it down the front of his shirt. He dabbed at the wet patch with his palm, then ran the hand through his hair.

"We're not here to harm you, Mr Presley," Derek said. "Quite the reverse in fact." He pulled an aged, yellowed newspaper from the black tube and held it towards Elvis. "Tomorrow's paper," he said.

Elvis took the newspaper and scanned the front page. When he looked back up at Derek there was another item for his inspection.

"Next month's *Rolling Stone*. There's quite a long article, obituary I guess, and you might notice your latest recording in the singles chart. The biggest hit you had for quite a while. Pity it had to be posthumous."

"I always wondered if you knew how much people were going to miss you, you might not have taken more care of yourself," Farrell said.

"There's no easy way to say this, Mr Presley, so I'll just come right out with it. In less than an hour you'll be dead. You were dying when we arrived. Mr Farrell has the antidote to the resuscitant we administered. It will erase all trace of our chemical intrusion."

"And you will die."

"But we've got an alternative for you."

"There can be a future for you."

"If you come with us. I know it's hard to believe. I know our evidence could all have been faked quite easily but I think you know that one thing we say is very definitely the truth. You know you are dying. At least, you knew it when you were slipping into unconsciousness. It was plain in your eyes." It was plain to Derek that Elvis was comprehending no more than half of what he was being told. It would have been so much easier just to lift him, but waking up in unfamiliar surroundings, in a world he neither knew nor understood, was likely to drive the remaining shreds of sanity from this pathetic husk. But even in his current sorry state, Elvis understood the dying part. Derek could read that much from him. Elvis would be rocking his way into the future tonight.

4th April 2154

Derek had that falling sensation in the pit of his stomach. He had known all along that finances were tight, but he had expected to get at least two years on the Morton Pinkney project. They were learning so much about the thought processes as well as the creative processes of the man who had become America's greatest cultural icon; the man whom critic Jerry Hopkins in the early 1970s called one of America's 'three best known contributions to the world.' The man who had become a 350lb hulk – then a corpse shot through with fourteen different drugs. It was too easy to blame his mother or Colonel Tom Parker or the death of his still-born twin, Jesse, or even the denial of his sex and drugs and junk food lifestyle.

The director's door stood open. Derek could hear Krause talking on the phone. He knocked and stuck his head into the room. Krause waved him inside and gestured at a chair in front of his desk.

"…yes, yes, we have five point seven guaranteed with another three in year two. If you can generate, say, two more I think we've got a green light." Krause placed a hand over the mouthpiece. "Won't be long. Washington," he said to Derek, then back into the mouthpiece. "That's fine, Peter. I can go with that. Let's pencil it in for…" he jiggled the mouse to clear the screen saver from his computer screen. "… how about the seventeenth?" He smiled. "Fine. I'll log that in. See you then. And you. Regards to Jackie."

Krause returned the handset to its cradle and swivelled to square up to Derek. "Charities," he said, casting his eyes to heaven.

Derek mumbled something which he hoped sounded appropriate and supportive.

"Now, Derek, there's no use beating around the bush. I'm sure you know why I asked you to call by."

Derek looked at him helplessly. He didn't want to answer. He didn't want to admit to the inevitability of Krause's message.

"I know it's a blow, Derek, but you can't claim to be totally surprised."

"Can't we keep it going for just another few months. Two, even. There's so much more to come."

"Sorry, Derek. You know this project was one of my babies so you know how much it hurts me to have to do this."

To himself Derek said, Yeah, sure. I'll bet the funding wouldn't have dried up half as quickly if we'd gone for Morrison like you wanted.

"Do you want to tell Pinkney we're cutting him loose, or would you prefer if I did it?"

Derek shook his head. "I'll break it to him."

"Good." Krause pushed his chair back and stood to indicate that the meeting was over.

"Hang on. What arrangements will we be making for him?"

"Arrangements?"

"We can't just throw him out into the street. Everything and everybody he knows has been dead for nearly two hundred years."

"He got a familiarisation programme and he's supposed to be this huge talent, isn't he? There'll be no problem for him getting a gig somewhere."

"Surely his estate wouldn't want to see him abandoned?"

"As far as they're concerned he died in August 1977. Their responsibility is to his heirs." Krause walked around the desk and took Derek by the arm. "Look, Derek, I've arranged ID for the Pinkney name that will stand up to the closest scrutiny and authorised a 10K credit line for him. He won't be penniless." Krause led him towards the door.

They wouldn't even be giving him his name; that belonged to his heirs. As did his image and his back catalogue. "But we can't just..."

"We can and we will, Derek, because we have to. The experiment is over. If we have insufficient data that's unfortunate, but the clinical subject must be disposed of. As always."

"He's not a subject, he's a man."

Krause shrugged. "Nothing I can do." He released Derek's arm. They were on opposite sides of the threshold. The closing door forced Derek to take a step backwards.

12th January 2157

It was an old poster. Looked like it had been stuck on the inside of the window for months. Derek's fiancée tugged at his arm. She was cold and she was anxious to get home. She could not understand what had caused Derek to stop outside this particular bar on this particular street. Surely he didn't expect her to go in there with him. Her mouth curled into obvious distaste. She looked like she had just discovered maggots in her salad.

"It couldn't be," Derek said.

"You're right, Derek, now let's go. I'm freezing."

"Just a minute. I've got to check something out."

"In there?"

"One minute, Carole. I promise."

She stared after him as he disappeared into the darkened interior. She looked at the poster. Who the hell was Morton Pinkney? She'd never heard of him. *One night only* sounded too long. And anyway, that one night had to have passed months ago. The poster was curling off the glass at the corners and had yellowed with exposure to daylight.

Carole was cold and annoyed by the time Derek reappeared. Stamping her feet had kept them from freezing completely but her knees, above the top of her boots but below the hem of her dress, were aching from the cold. Despite his enthusiastic smile Carole felt only misery. She was beyond being pleased for him.

Derek interpreted her pained expression in milliseconds. "Come on, love, we'd better get you out of this weather." He put an arm around her shoulder and hustled her towards a taxi rank. The door of the first cab in line hissed open on a wash of warm air. Carole's teeth continued to chatter as they glided homewards but her expression thawed. She would not want to return to the bar later, but she would not object too strongly to him going. Purely in the interests of science, naturally.

The MC wore a shiny black dinner jacket that had originally boasted a matt finish. His bow tie bore evidence of past dinners. He delivered a handful of coarse one-liners that the audience ignored and drew himself up dispiritedly to introduce the star turn. "Ladies and Gentlemen, it gives me immense pleasure to welcome back that long-time favourite of

the Cedars Lounge, the one, the only, the inimitable Morton Pinkney."
He clapped his hands over his head. "Give him a big hand, folks."

Derek clapped enthusiastically. For about three seconds. The resounding silence of the other patrons encouraged him to stop. He looked around the room. Nobody was paying any attention to the stage. The buzz of conversation remained unabated as Pinkney picked out the intro to *Don't Be Cruel* on the battered white piano. It was a slow, almost mournful version, bearing more resemblance to Billy Swan's countrified version that the king's original. *In The Ghetto* was next up, rendered as a straight ballad, and *You Were Always On My Mind* had acquired the phrasing and tempo of Willie Nelson's hit. It was as though the King needed to distance himself from his repertoire even while performing it.

The voice was smooth and controlled, the piano accompaniment was better than competent. There was even some feeling injected into some of the lyrics. But Derek was the only one listening. He signalled to a barman and ordered a drink for 'Mr Pinkney.' When it was delivered the barman nodded in his direction. The king raised the glass and saluted him. There was no recognition in eyes set deep in a bloated face.

During the course of the project they had knocked seventy pounds off his weight through diet and exercise. But all that good work was destroyed now. Derek watched the way he disposed of a succession of drinks during the set and reckoned it was probably the alcohol that had bloated him. But even in his state of physical decay he managed to put a special something into his performance, a mark of genius that no-one else was looking for or even heard. Despite the blanket of indifference that seemed to physically dampen the simple spell of piano and voice, Pinkney maintained an air of dignity. Even if the audience didn't care, his integrity would not allow him to merely go through the motions. He was performing for them as though each number was greeted with enthusiastic applause. His links were amusing and intelligent to begin with, poignant to finish.

Because there was no-one else listening, Pinkney began addressing the links directly to Derek. The first one caught him off guard, so he wasn't certain he heard it right. He thought it was, "This one's for my little girl, Lisa Marie." He was sure it ended, "I miss her so much."

171

He listened more carefully for the next one. "I guess it's too late to dedicate a number to my maw and paw, but I'm going to anyway." The archaic southern accent was beginning to break through as Pinkney became drunk, though his singing was unaffected and remained beautiful.

"I'm told this one was a hit," he said, introducing *Way Down*, "but it's a piece of crap and I don't know how I ever let them persuade me to record it. I guess I let them talk me into a whole heap of things back then. Other people always ran my life for me. I guess that's the way I liked it. Though maybe it was just I didn't know any better. I'm not sure. It was a long time ago in another world."

"Shut up and sing," somebody shouted.

"Hey, we've got a music lover in the audience," Pinkney said.

Derek laughed. He was the only one. The heckler staggered to the toilet, muttering something under his breath.

Pinkney smiled. It was sad and lonely. He looked over the top of the piano, directly at Derek. "Yep," he said, "somebody always ran my life. 'Cause I let 'em. But no more. I guess 'cause I got nothing you want any more."

He played *Way Down* at about half speed. It sounded awful, the first number all night that disappointed. Derek was sure it was meant to.

"Well, I guess it's time to say goodnight to all you good folks out there and especially to my good friend Derek Mills. Tell the boys, the King says hello."

Him addressing Derek like that from the stage was like a jolt of electricity down his spine. He had not realised Pinkney recognised or remembered him. He had thought himself a faceless shadow in the crowd. Derek thought he was talking to him because he was the only one interested.

He went straight into his final link. "I always like to end with something meaningful. Tonight it's the *American Trilogy*. I hope you like it, Derek." He began to sing. "I wish I was in the land of cotton…"

Derek had not realised how sad a human voice could sound. The message was for him. It could have been no clearer. His eyes filled with tears. Pity and shame is a strange cocktail. In the end Derek wasn't sure whether he was sorry for Pinkney or himself. Sorry for what the project had done to him. Sorry because it had been a futile experiment. Sorry because they had not been allowed to succeed. Sorry because he had been a party to playing God. Sorry for Pinkney's pain.

As the singer hummed over the final notes of the tune a woman stepped onto the stage and kissed his cheek. She was tall and slender and dressed expensively. Derek caught only a glimpse of her face. She was stunning. Beautiful in a way that takes the breath away. They slipped backstage hand in hand. In his haste to follow Derek knocked over his chair and sloshed the last of his drink across the table. There was nothing backstage except an unsanitary toilet and a room no bigger than a broom cupboard. The King had left the building.

For a while during the performance Derek had felt close to some of the secrets the Morton Pinkney project set out to learn. But the woman had thrown him. She didn't fit the picture he had built of a sad alcoholic wreck with a flickering, wasted talent. There was something about the way she carried herself, the way she possessed him in that short moment he saw them together, something that put Pinkney beyond the scientist's experience again. Once more he could really be the King; unknown and unknowable. A star. Capable of anything. His myth restored. If only to one man.

Faces I Remember

A battered Skoda van rattled slowly through the light afternoon traffic on the outskirts of Dresden. Its engine coughed sickly as the driver downshifted with an elongated grinding noise. A puff of thick black smoke jetted from the exhaust. The driver turned to the front seat passenger and cursed.

"Calm down, Harry," the passenger said.

"I am calm. Considering."

"There's a left turn up ahead. Take it."

On the corner a soldier leant his rifle against the wall to light a cigarette. As the Skoda turned the corner its passenger waved to the soldier.

"What are you doing, Stu?" the driver hissed.

"He waved back. Most natural thing in the world."

"How far now?"

"Revolution Boulevard is second on the right, about half a mile ahead."

Harry knocked on the window dividing the cab from the back of the van. "Just there," he called out.

"Pull in here," Stu said. As the van halted: "Blue door, three, four, five away."

Harry consulted his watch. "Twelve minutes ahead of schedule." He opened the door and stepped onto the pavement, stretching broadly.

Stu went to the back of the van and opened the doors. "Everybody okay?"

"You cut that a bit fine, Harry." A slender man in his early twenties slid his legs over the doorwell and let them swing.

"Twelve minutes grace, Commie," Harry said. "I haven't been late to a gig yet."

Commie lit a cigarette. A dark man, somewhat older, leaned over his shoulder and took the cigarette, dragging deeply. "If our intelligence is correct the subject will be home already," Commie said. "There's no point in hanging around longer than we have to. Let's get going." He stood and turned, leaning back into the van. Casually he straightened, a Colt automatic in his right hand. From his trouser pocket he produced a short fat cylinder that he screwed onto the barrel of the handgun. A fifth man jumped from the back of the van, a similar weapon in his left hand. The others all armed themselves from the van as Commie spoke quietly. "You all know the drill. Harry, start the engine as soon as we enter the house. Sarge take the back, Stu you cover the front, Macca and..."

Stu interrupted. "I want to go in this time. I'm always on lookout."

The older man chipped in, "It's always you and Macca doing the wet work. Go on, give him a go."

Harry nodded. "Yeah, give him a go." He smiled. "And me next time."

Macca shrugged, sliding his gun into the waistband of his trousers. "I'll take the front, Stu. You can go in with Commie." Without the gun in his hand, Macca looked like a choirboy, the one in any group of lads a girl would be happy to take home to meet her Mum. He didn't look as young as Harry, though youth was relative. Their eyes were cold and hard. War does that to young men.

"Doctor Weiss has a bodyguard," Commie said, "watches him every minute of the day and night."

"Jailer, more like," Macca observed.

"I'll take the guard. Stu, you take Weiss. Okay?"

Stu nodded, trying to look pleased but his face was pale and Commie thought he detected a slight tremor in his friend's hands.

"You sure you want to go through with this, Stu?"

Stu cleared his throat, controlling his voice long enough to emit a single word. "Yes."

"Right then. Places everyone. Sarge, you've got five minutes to get into position."

They smoked and counted the minutes. Commie ground his cigarette butt under his heel and Harry climbed into the cab of the van. The other two flanked Commie as they walked briskly to the house of their target. The door was opened by a tiny woman, in her fifties. Commie shot her through the forehead before she had time to speak. Macca took up a post in the doorway watching the street. Each of them had memorised the floor-plan of the house. Commie made straight for the study. It was empty. Next he went to the kitchen. Two men sat at the kitchen table drinking tea. When they saw the intruders the taller of the men, built like an all-in wrestler, stood abruptly, his chair skittering across the tiled floor. His hand reached inside his jacket. Commie shot him twice in the chest. The other man ran from the kitchen. A slight hesitancy on the part of Stu allowed him to escape the room.

"Shit!" Stu sprinted after him. Commie checked that the guard was dead and followed. The stairs to the upper floor of the house were back in the direction Weiss had fled. As Commie reached the bottom of the staircase he heard a cry of pain and surprise, then the thud of a body hitting the floor. Commie sprinted up the stairs, stopping at the first doorway. He glanced inside. Weiss was bent over the body of Stu, prising the gun from his lifeless grasp. A large kitchen knife protruded from Stu's throat. There was a lot of blood. Calmly, Commie emptied the rest of his clip into the doctor who tumbled limply onto Stu.

Rolling the doctor away from his friend, Commie went through Stu's pockets to make sure there was nothing to identify him as a member of Her Majesty's Armed Forces. There shouldn't have been, but then Stu shouldn't have been dead either. He found nothing. Stu's gun was traceable to a black market dealer in Rome. With the Italians' questionable loyalties it would serve to raise as many questions as it answered.

At the door he said to Macca, "Stu's dead." His voice was flat, devoid of emotion. They had a job to finish. He would grieve for his friend later.

It took the team a week to make their rendezvous point to the east of Potsdam on the Baltic coast. The only hairy moment occurred on the beach as they waited for the submarine to pick them up. A routine patrol had passed within twenty paces of their hideaway in the dunes. One of the patrol had stopped to answer a call of nature and had actually urinated on Sarge's pack. Even the Captain, 'Call me Brian, chaps,' had seen the funny side of it during debriefing. But he obviously sensed there was something amiss. Over the following week he seemed to keep a closer eye on them than usual. He always watched Commie closely –

"Fancies you, he does," Sarge always said.

"Likes his privates," as the joke inevitably went, this time from Harry. "But he prefers Commie's."

"Fuck off," Commie said, displaying his command of the language.

Like all insertion teams, Commie's crew were treated a bit like royalty. Exceptions were made for them. They didn't have to drill. None of them particularly enjoyed wearing uniform and except for formal occasions they were allowed to wear civvies. Their billet was sacrosanct: designed to hold eight, the hut was their own private domain. The officers turned a blind eye to their use of alcohol and on a Saturday night it was not unknown for one of the local *frauliens* to be smuggled into camp. If they were not engaged in an operation or in the planning phase they were left pretty much to their own devices. Consequently their billet was a popular drop-in spot amongst the men, though in the days since the Dresden gig visitors had been discouraged by Commie.

Most of the time he sat quietly smoking on his bunk, staring at the ceiling. Occasionally he would pull his guitar out of his footlocker and strum something bluesy. Whenever he bumped into American troops he would persuade them to sell him some of their records. He particularly liked the old Delta blues men, though he mainly played songs by more modern artists like Little Richard or Buddy Holly. It was a shame Holly was dead. Why did the Americans insist on drafting their stars? It wasn't like Holly had been much of a soldier. He only hoped Elvis didn't go the same way.

At least the Americans still had some kind of normal life back home. There was still music being made, and films and theatre and art. All the things that made life worth living. Commie had always wondered what might have happened if not for the war. Lots of people thought he had talent. He might have started a band himself. He absently began to pick out the guitar line to *That'll Be The Day*. Macca picked up the rhythm part and Harry began to weave some freeform variations around the theme. Sarge began to bang on the foot of his bunk with some cutlery in a crude, driving rhythm that eventually forced Commie to pick up the pace. After a while Macca began to sing. Harry threw in some harmonies and finally Commie picked up the vocal adding some words he had made up himself. They segued seamlessly into *Peggy Sue* and then into a song Macca had written which didn't have a name yet.

It was the first time since Stu's death that anyone had dared to have fun around Commie. They all knew he blamed himself. Stu had only been part of the team because he was their leader's mate. He had never really had a talent for killing like the others. He had learned how to handle a gun and had become pretty cool under fire, but with Stu it always seemed forced. He never looked comfortable on ops. Harry always felt Stu would have been happier if he had stayed in the camouflage unit where he started out. He had been a bloody good painter. But a crap killer. And now he was dead. And Commie blamed himself. And that was the sort of thing that could get them all killed on their next mission. Or the one after. Commie was the team leader. Hesitancy on his part could be fatal for them all, not just himself. They needed him firing on all cylinders.

Harry followed the music without conscious thought. They had moved on to a Bo Diddley number. There was a slot for a tasty solo coming up and it was about time he flexed his musical muscles. Macca was good on guitar, but preferred the piano when he could get one. When he couldn't he'd steal the lead parts if Harry wasn't quick enough off the mark.

The hut door opened, allowing a cold blast of November air inside. Commie began to let rip at the culprits even as he glanced up. "Shut that fuu...." He clamped down on the obscenity. There were officers in the house. One of whom he didn't recognise. He wore the insignia of a colonel.

Macca was first to his feet. "Atten... hut."

A clash of silence was followed by boots hitting the wooden floor.

"At ease men," Captain 'Call me Brian' said. "We heard the music from outside and Colonel Martin asked to look in. Hope you don't mind."

179

"Not at all, sir. The Captain is always welcome," Macca said. "And his guests."

Colonel Martin grinned. "From what I hear, it's quite an honour for an officer to be allowed in here."

The team forced laughter to humour the officer. No matter how special they might be in their own little pond, they could not afford to cross a colonel.

"Was that a Muddy Waters song I heard you playing as we came in?"

"Bo Diddley, sir," Macca answered. "Commie's a big fan."

"Commie?" Martin turned to the captain.

"Private Lennon, sir. They call him Comrade. You know, Comrade Lennon."

"I see. And you're the leader of this bunch, Comrade?"

"In the field, sir."

"And musically?"

"It's every man for himself, sir," said Harry.

"Before the Bo Diddley piece, I didn't recognise the song."

"One of our own, Colonel," Macca said proudly.

"You write?"

"Me and Commie, mostly."

"Perhaps the boys could play one for you, Colonel," the Captain said.

"I'd love to hear them," Martin said, "but I've got an appointment with the old man so I'd better cut along."

"A short one."

Martin shook his head. "Best be going."

*

Commie had his good days and his bad. The Russians made a push into what was left of Germany on the western side of the Iron Curtain and all incursion units were put on alert. But the Red Army retreated for its own unfathomable reasons before the Allies had formulated an appropriate response. There was talk that terror strikes were to be re-instituted. The thought of it plunged Commie into bleak depression. It was the one aspect of his job he could not come to terms with. Killing people like Doctor Weiss he could understand. Weiss's death could conceivably shorten the war. Anyone working on development of the A Bomb deserved to die anyway.

From what Commie had heard, The Bomb was an abomination. Not only would it wipe out entire cities at a stroke but it would eat away at the survivors afterwards for years. There were those who said that whoever got The Bomb first would win the war. Commie wanted nothing to do with that filth. Weiss got what he deserved. He could even justify killing the woman who answered the door; an unfortunate but necessary casualty of war.

But the terror strikes were a different matter. They had killed innocent men, women and even children. To frighten the civilian population. To show them that nobody was safe. The victims did not know what was going on. Commie would never forget the confusion in their eyes. They did not even know to plead for their lives. He would never forget their faces, now mixed in his memory with those of his friends and relatives. Strangers who would never change, whose faces would never grow older. He had written a song about them. But it was not for playing in public. Maybe he'd let the lads hear it. It would be interesting to hear Macca's opinion. Alone in the billet, he began to pick out the intro.

As he played with the unfinished tune there was a gentle knock at the door. It could only be Brian. He kept playing. "Yeah."

Brian came in and sat on the end of Commie's bed. His hands fluttered nervously, brushing imaginary lint from his shirt, smoothing the wrinkles from his battledress, adjusting his swagger stick as though searching for a place to hide it. Commie grinned, enjoying the officer's discomfort. He knew Brian fancied him and played on it. He knew he could slice the Captain's innermost self wide open with a few carefully chosen words. And if the shirtlifter said a word out of place this might just be his unlucky day. The sensation of having such power over another human being, particularly a toff like Brian who wouldn't look at him twice in civvy street, lightened his depression a little.

"Nice tune," Brian said. "What's it called?"

"*Murdered Innocents.*"

"Catchy."

Commie laughed. He had never really credited Brian with a sense of humour. "Wait 'till you hear the lyric. It's a doozy. Everyone I ever

181

murdered for Her Majesty is in there." He laughed again and shook his head. "Sorry. I'm a bit down. Feeling sorry for myself. Not your fault. Or your problem."

"But it is my problem. I can't send you into the field in this state. You'd just get the team and yourself killed."

"Is there a job for us."

"Not really. The yanks would like to borrow you for an op, but I said no."

"Why would the yanks want us?"

"Your record is really rather good. Anyway, at the moment you won't be going anywhere."

Commie tapped his temple. "You reckon I'm losing it? You could always invalid me out."

"What about the others. They wouldn't last a month without you."

"I didn't know you cared."

"I've grown fond of your little unit, Private Lennon. I kind of look on you as a family group."

"So you want to save us all, is that it?"

"Something like that."

"All or none."

"A bit like the opposition, eh Comrade?" Brian smiled.

Commie could almost like him like this.

"There might be a way to get you all out. Colonel Martin is setting up a concert party to tour the European theatre. He thought you and the boys had potential and he's arranging a little party for Saturday. I can get you on the bill. It will be a sort of audition."

Commie smiled. His depression was fading fast. A chance to get out of this horrible mess and to play in a band with his mates; what more could a bloke want?

"I guess we'd better start practicing then."

Saturday came quicker than any weekend in history. Commie couldn't believe how bad they sounded as a band. Sarge had played drums professionally before he joined up. But that had been eight years ago. It was a shame what the regular army could do to a man. Commie couldn't understand why anyone would join the army, especially with a war going on, hot or cold. Having been called up, Commie of course did his best to shirk until he had been put into the incursion team. Something clicked. He felt like he was home. It was a job he was good at, something he had never found before. He had always felt when he was growing up that he would be an artist or a writer or even a singer, but there was precious little chance of that with the Red menace on their doorstep. The yanks still had entertainers under forty, but they were a long way away from Russia. Unless you counted Alaska. And nobody really did.

Macca insisted they have a name and Sarge came up with The Privates. Commie nearly ruptured himself laughing. No-one could complain; they were privates. The set list kind of wrote itself: one by Little Richard, two by Buddy Holly and one by Macca and Commie. Sitting waiting to go on, a yank comedian stopped by. Macca recognised him from somewhere, but neither could remember where they had met.

"Nervous, fellas?" the yank was likeable but smiled too much.

"Naw," Sarge said, holding out hands that defined palsy.

"I thought you guys were a live ops unit?"

"We are."

"You'll be on the big push then."

"Big push?"

"Our guys are talking about nothing else. Tuesday is going to be the big one."

"We've heard nothing," Commie said. "Too busy practising."

"What are you guys, artillery was it? Nooo…"

"Incursion unit."

The yank stopped smiling. "Jesus H. Christ, man, I'm sorry."

"Sorry for what?" Harry asked.

"I don't want to be the one to tell you."

"But I think you'd better." Commie spoke very softly. The team were immediately on edge. He set his guitar against the side of the chair. There was violence in the air. The threat was palpable.

The yank got the idea, more from the reaction of the others than what Commie said or how he said it. The one who had put his guitar down looked like a mean son-of-a-bitch, the sort who would gut you without a second thought. Not a guy to cross. "The incursion units are going in first. Every one of them. Their brief will be to cause as much mayhem as possible before the actual attack. Get the Russkies running around, chasing their tails."

"So?" Commie let the word hang in the air.

The yank cleared his throat then coughed, pulling at his collar. He cleared his throat a second time. "Casualties are expected to be high."

"How high?" Macca asked.

"I heard the figure eighty percent would be sustainable."

"What does sustainable mean?" Commie asked.

"It means they don't see much use for Incursion Units after Tuesday."

Nobody spoke for a while.

The yank said, "Sorry guys."

"Wasn't your idea," Commie said. A pause, then, "Was it?"

The yank barked a mirthless laugh and left. Five minutes later The Privates were on stage.

Their set lasted twelve minutes and thirty seconds, two and a half minutes below their allotted time. They got a decent round of applause when they finished but none of them felt they had done themselves justice. Brian patted them all on the back and enthused; good for the ego if nothing else. They were all surprised when Colonel Martin appeared.

"Private Lennon," the Colonel said, "Can I have a few words?"

He led Commie to one side. "I think you have potential, Lennon. You wrote that last song?"

"Macca helped with the melody. He's good at that."

"I might be able to fit him in as well. Listen, I've no time to talk now, but my CO is out there and I've got to get back to him. I'm pushing to get you included in our concert party but he's not convinced. So I've got you another slot. Enough for one song. Something poppy. Catchy. He likes Paul Anka. Do you know *Wooden Heart*? Anyway, you're on in five minutes. When the next act finishes."

"We're a package deal. A group. Mates. Not a solo act."

"You and Macca. At a push. Not the others. No way." He turned to leave then stopped, glanced back over his shoulder. "Have you heard about the show on Tuesday?"

"Yes."

"Need I say more?"

John knew there was no point in talking to the others. Sarge and

Harry would tell him to go for it. Macca would insist they should stick together. But this was his moment, his decision. Martin didn't really want Macca either. Just him. He picked up his guitar and headed for the stage as the last act filed off.

Private Lennon appeared very small and skinny in the spotlight all by himself. He shaded his eyes and tried to make out Colonel Martin, but the glare was too much for his poor eyes. He tapped the mic to ensure it was live. "This is a catchy little tune I wrote. It's sort of autobiographical. Big word for a private that. But I won't bore you any more with my chatter. I call this one *Murdered Innocents* and it's for Colonel Martin."

He played two phrases of introduction then began to sing.

"There are faces I remember..."

Tales of Far Americay

A small, soft fist knocked gently on the door of Johnny Power's cottage. He recognised the sound; it could only be little Aoife. "Don't be standing there on the doorstep all day," he called. "You're making the place look untidy."

The door creaked open and three children entered. They stood just inside the door, blinking as their vision adjusted to the gloom of the interior. The cottage's windows were tiny, and even in the height of summer admitted little sunlight. On an overcast winter's day it was close to pitch black. Johnny smiled at his niece's brood, cocking a quizzical eyebrow towards their companion.

"This is Geoffrey," Killian said, pushing the other boy forward into the circle of illumination cast by a turf fire, so that his great uncle could see clearly. "Doctor Shiner's son," he added by way of qualification.

"Ah!" Johnny said, nodding. Carrakill was not big enough to warrant a doctor of its own and once a fortnight Doctor Shiner made his way up from Killorglin to hold surgery in the upstairs room of Langan's pub.

The doctor had brought the boy before, if he was on holiday from school and under his mother's feet, but this was the first time the youngster had ventured away from his father's care. "Sit down, sit down," he said, waving an arm towards a huge, old, broken-down couch, which leaked stuffing like heavy snow clouds.

A large birdcage hung on a wooden stand to the left side of Johnny's chair, away from the fire. The door stood open and its occupant, a mynah bird as big as a crow and plump as a Christmas turkey, stood guard on the back of its master's chair. "Good afternoon," the bird said, flapping its wings as though in greeting.

The children sat, turning expectant faces up to the old storyteller, although Geoffrey initially seemed more interested in the mynah. Uncle Johnny Power sat back into his chair and began to tamp his pipe with a calloused thumb. He smiled and stuck it in the side of his mouth. "I expect you've come for a story," he said rhetorically. "Was there anything in particular you had in mind?"

Killian looked at the Doctor's son who shrugged. Aoife wriggled slightly forward on the couch and cleared her throat.

"Yes, love?" Johnny said.

"You've told us lots of adventures and things but I'd really like to hear about how you went to Americay and what it was like when you arrived and that sort of thing."

Somehow it sounded to Johnny like a prepared speech. He was almost certain the words weren't her own. "Are you sure? There's a great story I haven't told you about a Skraeling chief and a Viking princess."

Both Killian and Aoife looked to their guest.

Geoffrey furrowed his eyebrows. "No. Something real," he said. "Like the journey to Americay."

Had one of the village children been so rude as to suggest that not all of Johnny's stories were one hundred percent fact, he'd have thrown them out of the cottage without ceremony. But it was obvious that Killian and Aoife were intent on impressing their new friend and he didn't want to disappoint them. He reached his hand above his head to the mantelpiece and took a spill from an earthenware jar. Bending over, he lit the spill from the fire and began to puff his pipe into life. As a thick pall of grey smoke began to build, the old man tilted his head back slightly and began to speak, as if addressing the blackened ceiling. The mynah bird made repeated harsh sounds in its throat and blinked concern at the old man.

*

"In the year of Our Lord, Nineteen Hundred and Forty Seven," Johnny began, "I turned my back on the village of Carrakill to see what the wide world had to offer me. I was almost twenty-five years of age and I had never been further than Killarney. On my back I had a pack which held all my worldly goods: a change of clothes, a tin whistle and a bible.

"Heading south through the Reeks, I walked to Kenmare whence I took an omnibus to Cork and from there another one to Cobh. There, I sat for hours and stared in wonder at the seemingly endless stream of ships that sailed through the harbour. Iron-sided, Yankee steamers laden with cotton and tobacco and slaves from the new world, funnels belching thick, black smoke. Sleek Vinland clippers with their proud demon's head prows, filled to the gunwales with wheat and maize and dried beef.

"I had no money so my plan was to work passage on one of these transatlantic giants. Perhaps one trans-shipping automobiles from Great Britain or the continent. I spent four hungry days that felt like four weeks trying to find a berth on a ship bound to New York. Eventually I was taken on by the captain of a small merchantman carrying farm machinery. I thought it an odd cargo for New York but said nothing as I was desperate to find a berth. He needed a galley hand as the cook's assistant had fallen ill and would have to be left in Cobh to recover.

"I had, even in the depths of the Macgillicuddy's Reeks, heard of seasickness. I had even supposed that it was likely to affect me. What I had not imagined was the severity of the malady. For the rest of the trip I spent more time in my bunk or with my head stuck out a porthole than I did in the galley. A less understanding man than the cook I was supposed to assist would probably have petitioned the captain to have me thrown overboard. There were times when I wished he had."

"I'll bet there were," said Aoife, with a shudder. "I don't ever want to go on a ship."

"You don't ever want to do anything except stay in Carakill and marry Peadar Spillane," Killian said.

"That's not true," Aoife protested.

"When I'm grown up I'm going to take off for Americay like Uncle Johnny," Killian continued, ignoring his sister. "Except I won't be coming back to this..."

An elbow spearing him in the ribs stopped his gallop. "Take that back," Aoife demanded, the hint of a wail in her voice. "You know I don't even like Peadar Spillane."

"You do so. I saw you sitting with him in Church last Sunday but one, and you holding his hand."

"Don't you say another word," Aoife yelled.

"Children, children," Johnny said, a patient smile on his face. "There's no call for this. Let's all settle back down. Maybe what we need is another sort of tale. One with a little more fun in it."

Johnny Power was uneasy telling stories about himself, especially with a stranger present. He was also unused to steering a course so close to the facts. But he felt that he owed at least that much to Killian and Aoife. The Doctor's son was another matter. The boy sat in silence and stared at Johnny with a trace of what could have been derision on his lips, as though weighing up the old man and finding him wanting. He had seen octogenarians with more naiveté and trust. It would be easier by far for him to return to a well-honed and trusted fiction considering the critic in the audience. He could tell his niece's children the story of his journey another time. Any other time.

"Sorry for messing, Uncle Johnny," Killian said. "Don't stop. We'd really love to hear this through to the end. You haven't even got to Americay yet."

"Please continue, Mr Power," Geoffrey said, smiling as though at a secret. "This really is very entertaining."

"Yes, Uncle Johnny," Aoife said, in her most winning tone. "Please?"

The Shiner boy sounded like he'd swallowed a dictionary, Johnny thought. On the back of his chair, the mynah bird screeched. It sounded almost like an admonition. The old man threw a dark glance at his feathered companion before somewhat reluctantly continuing the story.

"Where was I?" he asked.

"Somewhere in the middle of the Atlantic, wishing you were dead," Killian reminded him.

"Nearly at New York?" Aoife enquired excitedly.

"Well," Johnny said, "this story isn't really about Americay."

All three children sat up a little straighter, puzzlement on their faces. Johnny was glad to see Geoffrey looking more like a child and a little less like a member of the Inquisition.

*

"You see," Johnny said, "the ship wasn't going to New York as I'd been told. Nor was the cargo farm machinery. So I discovered when I innocently remarked to one of the crew on how cold it was getting. He must have presumed I was in the know.

"'It'll be getting a lot colder before Newfoundland,' he said. I had great difficulty not blurting out my surprise. We were leaning on the rail staring out into the great banks of fog that drifted by. He was probably on watch for icebergs or the like. 'We're not actually putting ashore in Newfoundland, though,' I said, trying to sound casual.

"'Of course not. We'll be making rendezvous with the Skraelings about five miles out. There's no way the captain'd take a chance of landing on Vinish territory with a cargo like that.'

"I was totally confused. I laughed. 'They don't much like ploughs.'

"'Especially semi-automatic ploughs in the hands of insurrectionists,' he chuckled, continuing the thread of what he thought was my joke.

"I bade him goodnight and moved farther along the rail to empty my stomach in peace. The realisation that I'd got myself mixed up with a bunch of gun-runners brought on a relapse of my *mal de mer*."

"*Mal de mer?*" Aoife asked.

"Seasickness," Geoffrey explained. "It's French."

He definitely sounded smug. It wasn't just that Johnny simply didn't like him. He was sorry that he'd subjected the girl to Geoffrey's show of superiority. Why was he trying to show off to an eleven year old? Why was he letting the youngster get to him?

"What happened next, Uncle Johnny?" Killian asked, sounding a little annoyed at the interruption.

"Next?" Johnny said. "Well, three days later we rendezvoused with the Skraeling vessel in a fog so thick it took us two hours sailing round in circles before we could find them. Like yourselves I had heard tales of this fierce and proud race of warriors, but I had thought that if I ever saw one it would be on the streets of New York, wearing a suit and maybe a Derby hat. But here on the wide ocean, as they threw across their grappling hooks and pulled us alongside, their quiet determination seemed far more frightening than their reputation as warriors. In silence their aspect was fierce. Coal black hair worn long and decorated with bone and shells. And not all of the bone looked to be animal's. Dark sun-reddened skin and broad faces, they reminded me almost of the Mongols in the kingdom of Russia I had seen pictured in books. Despite the cold only some of them wore furs. Several stood about the decks bare-chested, traditional war paint smeared across their ribs. I'm sure that was for effect. It was probably their way of ensuring the gunrunners thought twice about cheating them.

"I retreated to the galley suspecting that there could well be discussions regarding the quality of the goods and the price. It struck me that blood was a currency which both sides dealt in."

*

"Were you scared?" asked Aoife.

"Sshhh!" Killian hissed. "Don't interrupt."

Tears welled in the little girl's eyes.

"It's all right, child," Johnny laughed, holding his arms out.

She climbed out of the couch and went to sit on his knee. The old man hugged her fondly. "I'm afraid your old Uncle Johnny Power was about the scaredest man on either of those boats," he said.

Geoffrey stared hard at him, uncertainty creeping into his eyes. The story was the sort of high-adventure fiction he had expected but where was Johnny Power, Hero?

"Being scared probably saved my life," Johnny went on. "Because somehow the deal did go sour. One minute boxes of weapons were being passed from one vessel to the other and the next guns were being fired off all over the place. The captain fell in the first exchange and our crew were beaten from the start. I was at the opposite end of the ship from the fighting and the Skraelings probably weren't even aware of my presence. Stopping only to pull an inflatable life raft and survival pack out of a locker, I slipped over the side into the freezing waters of the Atlantic.

"In the fog I got away unseen. Of course, I couldn't tell where I was going and even if I could, there was probably nothing to see except ocean. Which is how it was when the fog cleared. Unfortunately, I had not thought about charts or a compass, and you don't learn much about navigating by the stars or the sun working in the galley. So I was lost. Completely and totally.

"And lost I stayed. For nine days. Sometimes I rowed, mainly I just drifted. What was the point in using energy to row in what could have been the wrong direction? The current was as likely to take me toward land as not. The few scraps of rations lasted six days – mainly because most of the time I was too seasick to eat. At least I had no problem with water. It rained most days, most of the time. It was easy to fill a container. Keeping dry was impossible.

"On the ninth day I was picked up by a flying machine, a huge airship hundreds of feet in length with a cabin slung underneath, the size of a small trawler. The dirigible, as I later learned that type of machine was called, was powered by four enormous propellers that looked as though they'd been carved from whole oak trees. I could hardly believe my eyes when it appeared across the horizon. I had not known that such machines existed, or even that they were possible."

"A flying machine?" Geoffrey said, clearly disbelieving.

Killian and Aoife looked at old Johnny expectantly.

"This all happened in 1947," Geoffrey said. "But if I'm not mistaken the first powered flight didn't take place until 1954."

"The first recorded flight," Johnny replied.

The doctor's son smirked. A look passed between the boys. Aoife shifted uneasily on his knee.

Johnny ploughed on with the story attempting to generate excitement in his nephew's children at least. "The incredible machine hovered over me and a rope ladder dropped from it. It crossed my mind that it might be safer to stay in the boat but I was more afraid of the sea than of what might await me above. At the top of the ladder, a figure beckoned. I started up the ladder towards the door in the rear of the cabin where I was helped inside by a short Skraeling with only one arm, dressed in a field grey uniform the like of which I had not seen before. I thanked him effusively but he stared back stone-faced. 'Come,' he said.

"The Skraeling shut over the hatch and led me through what was obviously a storeroom onto the flight deck. There I saw three more

Skraelings and a huge blond man in late middle age who, in spite of a tight haircut and a beardless face, was undoubtedly a Viking. All four wore uniforms similar to that of my one-armed guide.

"The Viking's was a little more elaborate; with gold braid at throat and cuffs. He stood and held out his hand in greeting. 'Captain Anders Magnusson at your service,' he said in perfectly accented English. 'Sit down and tell me all about your adventures.' He indicated a bank of four armchairs surrounding a knee-high table. I noticed all the furniture was bolted to the floor. He said something in rapid Vinish to the one-armed Skraeling and the helmsman before giving me his undivided attention.

"Feeling that I was an innocent victim of circumstance I decided it was best to tell the truth. During my story Magnusson questioned me closely about what I had seen of Cobh; the harbour and its traffic. It was only natural for him to show interest, Cobh being the main destination in Europe for New World merchant ships. When I finished I was still unsure whether the good captain believed me or not."

The children stirred uneasily. Johnny watched the young outsider exert a strange power over his niece and nephew. It could be just that they were growing up, growing out of the magic that he wove with his tales. But Johnny could not afford to give up the fight for them. They were all he had. The only ones who loved him. The ones that made what was left to him worthwhile.

"For ages," Johnny went on, speeding up his delivery, "the captain stared at me as though trying to make up his mind whether he should deliver me up to the authorities or just throw me over the side. The one-armed Skraeling appeared from the storeroom skilfully balancing a laden tray on his single hand. He slid it onto the table before us.

"'Thank you, White Bear,' Magnusson said. The Skraeling saluted and turned to other duties.

"Without formality the captain set me to the food which was wholesome though somewhat poorly prepared. To accompany me Magnusson nibbled at some cheese and drank a little wine. While I demolished the remainder of the fare without difficulty, my rescuer talked.

"'By your accent, you are Irish,' he said. 'And Johnny... may I use your given name?' he asked, to which I nodded, my mouth being otherwise occupied. 'And Johnny, you have not the look of a sailor and your words have the ring of truth to them. So, it seems to me that you have been cast adrift on the sea of fate, as I myself have been.'

"I stopped shoving food into my mouth and stared at him, chewing hard to make space for a question. The captain smiled.

"'As you can see, my crew consists entirely of Skraelings, as you people call them. They prefer Native Vinlanders, themselves,' he explained. 'My own people have shunned me for most of my adult life because of my meddling in things that they consider best left untouched,' he said bitterly. A sweeping motion of his arm encompassed the whole airship in his statement. 'Too many people in the world are not prepared to accept the evidence of their own eyes. Most of them think that scientists are still searching for the philosopher's stone. Anything new is suspect. Anything as radical as flight can only be achieved by something akin to magic. Nothing as simple as engineering would be acceptable as an explanation.'

"I nodded, swallowing a large gobbet of Atlantic salmon. This was not the time to express my agreement with his countrymen's sentiments.

"Captain Anders Magnusson threw back his head and laughed. Something had amused him greatly. He slapped his right knee repeatedly with his right hand and continued to laugh until tears ran down his face and his breathing became short. He stopped, gasping for air, a broad smile still etched onto his face. 'I watched your rescue through my telescope,' he said. 'I only wish that there were a camera that could take pictures at such a range, so that you could see your face. Had I swooped down from the clouds riding on the back of a dragon I don't think you would have been any more reluctant to accept rescue.'

"I saw the funny side and began to laugh. Magnusson joined in, though not so heartily as before. 'Well boy,' he chuckled, 'it would seem to me that you might be in need of a job, what with all your worldly possessions lost when you abandoned ship. If you'd work for a magician, I'd be glad to have you. If not, I'll get you to the Vinish mainland as soon as I possibly can.'

"'Where are we headed now?' I asked.

"'Greenland,' he replied. 'That's where I make my home these days. It's difficult enough, even there, to go about my work undisturbed.' The captain drained his wineglass. 'Johnny,' he continued, 'after hearing you tell your story you strike me as a man with an eye for detail and a memory to go with it. I could use someone like you.'

"'To do what?'

"'To go to New York and walk about with your eyes and ears open. To see all the sights that you always wanted to see. To keep me in touch with what's going on. I think I can trust you to answer me honestly.'

"'That's a job?' I said, disbelieving my ears.

"'Yes,' he replied.

"'And you'll pay me to do it?'

"'Yes,' he repeated.

"'You'll pay me to go to New York and just tell you what the latest news is?' I was having difficulty believing that anyone could be stupid enough to offer to pay someone for such a service.

"'Once you've learnt what to look and what to listen for. Yes,' he said. 'Of course, it won't always be that easy getting your news to me and there may be some danger involved from time to time in collecting the data that I require.'

"Despite mention of difficulty and danger, which is easy to dismiss unless you're right in the middle of it, I decided to accept quickly, before he had time to rethink and withdraw the offer. I was going to New York. What I didn't realise was that it would be almost eighteen months before Captain Magnusson considered me trained for the task of intelligence gathering. An eighteen month apprenticeship amongst the wonderful machines that were crammed into his Greenland base. Other feats of engineering that he said would someday make him a rich man; someday when the world was ready for them.

"It would be twenty years before he deemed the time was right for introducing the ornithopter to the world. I'm still waiting to see his sun-powered car appear and the thing he called air pictures. Like radio it is, except you can see people as well as hear them. Sort of a small version of the Kinetoscope films you can see in the big cities. I often wondered; was Captain Magnusson the genius he portrayed himself to be, or were there others behind him? I worked for him for almost forty years and I never could decide."

The sun had moved past the cottage's small windows. Outside, early evening shadows were beginning to lengthen. Aoife had begun to fidget nervously on Johnny Power's knee. Killian sat picking at his nails, head down. Occasionally the two of them would look toward Geoffrey, checking his reaction. The doctor's son stared directly into the storyteller's eyes, a faintly amused smile on his lips. Johnny felt as though roles had been reversed and he was an eleven-year-old faced with the world weary scepticism of an adult in whom he had confided a belief in fairies. What was worse, the outsider's attitude had infected his niece's children.

Normally Killian and Aoife would be demanding that he continue for just another five minutes. Or they would be peppering him with questions about Greenland or Captain Magnusson or the machines he had hinted at. But not today. Today they seemed agitated, almost embarrassed. He lifted Aoife down from his knee and slid forward in his seat to poke some life back into his fire.

"I think it's about time you were going home for your tea," Johnny said. "And you, Geoffrey, I'm sure you're father will be finishing up pretty soon, if he isn't already."

"Yes of course, Mr Power," Geoffrey said. He went to the cottage door, the other children in his wake. He opened it and ushered them through.

Johnny could see that Aoife felt awkward at not giving him his usual kiss goodbye. It would be better if he didn't make an issue of it.

Geoffrey stood in the doorway, bathed in the dying rays of the sun.

"Thank you, Mr Power," he said, "for a most..." the pause was just long enough to squeeze the maximum of insolence into the next word, "...interesting afternoon." There was a look in his eye that seemed to say: We must do this again sometime. You can tell me where you really were during all those years you claimed to have spent in Americay. Turning to place his arms about the shoulders of his new friends, Geoffrey flicked the door shut with his heel.

Johnny Power stood up from his seat and bent over the basket of turf at the hearthside. The mynah bird danced across the back of his chair and squawked loudly in his ear.

"Don't say I didn't try to warn you," the mynah said.

"Shut up," Johnny replied succinctly. He threw a couple of sods onto the fire, raising a shower of sparks. Ash and embers were thrown past the grate to land on the hearthrug. The old man stamped on them vigorously.

"Temper, temper," the bird admonished.

"If you don't shut your beak this second, I'm going to squash you flat like I should have done years ago."

"The Captain wouldn't like that."

"So what? I don't work for him any more, I'm not answerable to him and I don't need you."

"And who's going to protect you if you get rid of me?"

"Protect me!" Johnny forced a laugh. "Protect me from what? The villagers would be more likely to burn me for witchcraft if they found out about you, than anybody else is to do me any harm."

"There are still those that would see you dead. You made enemies working for the Captain. You think I wouldn't be more use to him elsewhere? You think Magnusson'd leave me here defending you if you didn't need it? He may be sentimental but he's not a fool."

The old man sighed and returned to his seat. He was too tired and too dispirited to argue. "Maybe you're right," he said quietly.

"Of course I'm right," it replied. The machine lifted back to its cage without benefit of its wings. There was no need to expend energy on artifice if there was no-one around to appreciate it. "Shall I secure the cottage perimeter?"

"No," Johnny said. "Not yet. It's not quite dark. One or other of the children might drop back up when they get rid of young Shiner."

"Yes," the mynah said. Sometimes it was better to humour the old man.

Previously from Elastic Press

Going Back by Tony Richards

Time is of the essence, and in these fourteen stories from acclaimed horror writer Tony Richards the essence of time is the link that pulls his characters together. Richards explores the nature of reality and perception filtered through the conduit of time; examines how our decisions can lead us down unsettling paths, and however carefully we make our choices they can still contain strange consequences, often tragic ones.

A terrific story-teller – Graham Joyce

Forthcoming from Elastic Press

The Cusp of Something by Jai Clare

Jai Clare's stories are filled with the disaffected, those who kick against their everyday lives, who crave the mystic when seeking their spirituality, and who are desperate to be alone as much as they are desperate to be with someone. Finding meaning in the universal and the personal, through transient sex or emotional depth, her characters stand on the brink of discovery, laid bare to misfortune and fortune.

A courageously inventive writer – Jim Crace

For further information visit:
www.elasticpress.com

The British Fantasy Society exists to promote and enjoy the genres of fantasy, science fiction and horror in all its forms. We are well supported by the publishing industry and have many well known authors among our members, not least our president, Ramsey Campbell, who says: "This is an invitation to you to join the community of the fantastic. Many years ago, when I was a struggling writer and a vociferous fan, I tried to convince people that we admirers of fantasy needed a society to bring us together for fun and for sharing our ideas, and I don't know of a better such organisation than the British Fantasy Society..."

We hold regular Open Nights which are open to all, not just our members, and these are listed on our website, http://www.britishfantasysociety.org.uk, as well as in our bi-monthly news magazine, *Prism*. We also publish a bi-annual fiction magazine, *Dark Horizons*. Once a year, we hold our main convention, FantasyCon, an event that is always well attended by known and unknown alike. Recent Guests of Honour include Clive Barker, Neil Gaiman, Raymond E. Feist, Juliet E. McKenna, Robert Holdstock, Steven Erikson, not to mention our president, Ramsey Campbell.

Subscriptions: £25 (UK), £30 (Europe), £45 (Rest of World)p.a. Membership entitles you to six free issues of Prism, two of Dark Horizons, and free copies of all BFS Special Publications, also discounted attendance at BFS events. Cheques should be made payable to: British Fantasy Society, The British Fantasy Society, 36 Town End, Cheadle, STAFFS, ST10 1PF England. Or you can join online at the BFS Cyberstore: http://www.britishfantasysociety.org.uk/shop/info.htm.